THE GOD-MEN CLAN

Yogi

notionpress.com

INDIA • SINGAPORE • MALAYSIA

ISBN 979-8-88684-697-3

Ohm Ganapathaye namaha.
Ohm Namah Shivaya.
Ohm Saravana bhavaya.
Kottravai potri, kandha potri, iraiva potri.
Nadhan thaazh potri.
Potri, potri, potri.

Contents

Chapter 01: A Day in a Nomad's Calendar 7
Chapter 02: Men of Kurinji 11
Chapter 03: Fire and Dance 17
Chapter 04: The Sadhu Caves 23
Chapter 05: Painting a Destiny. 29
Chapter 06: The Waterfall 41
Chapter 07: Sun Scorched 49
Chapter 08: The Swamp and a Bunch of Swords 59
Chapter 09: Dungeons and Death Traps. 67
Chapter 10: The Sea, the Guards, and the Howling Wind 79
Chapter 11: Ferries and Folk Lore. 85
Chapter 12: Freedom and Slavery. 91
Chapter 13: The Blue and the Pearl 99
Chapter 14: Buying Freedom 109
Chapter 15: Red, Black, Blue, and Brown. 115
Chapter 16: Mortals, Mother Kottravai and the Muni's Return. 123
Chapter 17: The Clan of Gods 135

Chapter 18: Mystery Statue, Mindful Ignorance and Meticulous Plans 145
Chapter 19: Spies at Work 161
Chapter 20: Crashing a Party 171
Chapter 21: Guessing Game Ends 191

Chapter 01

A Day in a Nomad's Calendar

He didn't mean for the day to be any more productive than it turned out to be. The plan for the day was to climb the Palani hill. Even then, he didn't expect to reach the summit before afternoon. It was a pretty small hill, after all. He couldn't blame it on the hill though; from where he came, every hill seemed small. His mountain had to be the tallest summit he'd ever been on. He stood there on the summit not knowing what to do. The view was pretty enticing and promised a really good sunset, so he stood there, waiting for the sunset, at bright noon. He set his bag and glider down and used his spear to support his body weight. Should he sleep until the sun set? Should he eat something? What to do?

Should he sing? There was no one around; he could even dance. He finally decided that he was too lazy to do any of those things, and simply stood there. He was wearing nothing but a strip of white animal hide to cover his bare essentials, for it was too hot for him.

He usually wore the most clothes back home – where he came from – but as he moved farther down south, the climate got too hot to wear anything.

He stood there and stood there and stood there. He had nothing to do, really. He would simply wait for the sunset.

After waiting for what seemed like an eternity, the sun finally began to drop. He sat down to savour this feeling. He'd watched countless sunsets, from countless summits. He'd remember every single one of them, forever. He thought back to when his father first took him to the Sarikhanda summit, near his village, to watch a sunset. Just for that and nothing else. Ever since his love for watching a sunset had never dimmed. He actually liked the sunrise more than the sunset, but he never woke up in time. The sun slowly dropped into the clouds, pierced through them and came down, sinking into the horizon, as if a ball of fire had been dropped into a puddle of feathers. He forgot to breathe and didn't exist for the next few minutes. He was entranced by the show Mother Nature had put up for him.

There, what a fruitful day. As the sun went down, he planned to go downhill and sleep for the rest of the day. He had to bathe and wash his animal hide tomorrow. How long had it been?

He bathed last in the river near the Mahadeshwara mountain ranges. He had a pretty good time climbing the peak of that hill too. He took his bag and slung it across his shoulders. He tied it to his back and put his spear behind him as well. He then picked up his glider, taking a good look at its colour. Even after ten years, it had stayed intact. He and his father had spent three days adding drop after drop of blue, green, violet, and countless other colour dyes to create this shade. In broad daylight, it shined a beautiful peacock green. On dark nights, it seemed almost pitch black. His father was a genius designer and a true artist for painting it the way he had.

He held it together with both his hands. He then twisted two of the four knobs under the glider to bring out the two little wings, and dove right down the cliff.

Besides sunsets, this was the main reason he climbed mountains – so he could just jump off them and glide! The feeling exhilarated him so much that he never wanted to come down. His hair hung just below his chin and fluttered around as he flew through the trees and valleys. In a couple of minutes, he landed. He missed the long flights from his village, which stood at the top of the mountain, to its foothills that lasted for a solid eight to nine minutes. These mountains, however, weren't as tall. He found a decent spot for him to camp in and lit a campfire. After gathering some twigs to keep the fire going through the night, he started eating. He'd hunted this deer yesterday and could probably keep it until tomorrow, if he was lucky. If not, he'd have to hunt again or gather something to eat for his breakfast.

As he nibbled on his dinner, he went over his day once — he ate, he walked, he ate, he slept, he saw the sunset, he glided, and now, he was eating again.

"Wow," he muttered to himself as he finished his meal. "It's been a busy day."

He turned his glider down and pulled the other two knobs, pushing the four wings to make them point downwards. He now had his makeshift bed. He rarely slept on the bed, to his dismay. He'd usually wake up ten or fifteen feet away from where he slept. He'd never sleep with anyone near him as well, otherwise, he'd have to spend the entire of the next day listening to them bicker about him kicking them in his sleep. He would bathe tomorrow, he resolved. And wash his animal hides too.

The next day, he woke up and found a small stream, one that cascaded as a waterfall, quite a distance from where he was. He put on his tiger hide and washed everything else he owned. He decided to bathe after all the hides dried up so that he would be fresh. Just then, he heard a big thud, like a tree falling, and a few women screaming. He ran up to the ledge to see an animal chasing them.

"No, man. No. This was supposed to be my spa day!" he muttered before he took his every belonging and jumped down with his glider.

Chapter 02

Men of Kurinji

Valli walked in on a worried father and a furious chief.

"This long to gather a few fruits, Valli? I told you not to hunt or gather anything other than a few mangoes," he started but froze in his place. The blood on his face drained as he saw the huge black silhouette. He had seen one as a little boy, but never alive. Valli put out her hands to stop her father from instinctively issuing orders to get the village into a defensive stance. Who knew what would happen if the animal got all riled up again?

The chief was confused but looked a little closer at the animal, trying to get a good look at the boy playing behind one of its legs.

"We were ambushed by this Yaazhi in its musth. That boy saved us. We dropped all the fruit we'd gathered till then, and had to pick it all up again. That is the reason for the party being late, father. We're sorry," said Valli.

As she narrated what had transpired to her father, it hit her that she had just escaped death by inches. She burst into tears and hugged her father.

Nambirajan could not believe what he was seeing or hearing. A small part of his brain remembered to feel eternally grateful to all of the Gods in every heaven possible that his daughter was unharmed. He still could not believe that a Yaazhi was walking towards his settlement.

A few metres before the settlement, the Yaazhi stopped. The boy looked at it and called it a couple of times. When it hesitated to walk any further, he simply left the fruits he had in his hands down by the Yaazhi, and walked towards Valli and her father.

"Hello, Ayya."

The boy had learnt that the people who lived down south did a traditional namaskar by folding their hands, similar to what the people back home did to pray. They didn't touch their feet the way his people would. He couldn't decide which one to do, so whenever he met someone close to his age, he did the hand thing, and whenever he met an older person, he did both. Since Nambi looked like he was the boy's father's age, he walked a little closer to touch his feet. Valli sprung a little further away.

"Let you live a long, happy life, my son," an overwhelmed Nambi said, his voice breaking a little towards the end. He pulled the boy up and hugged him.

"You have saved my daughter, my boy. You have saved a lot of lives along with hers. As a father and the chief of the village, I am indebted to you. I owe you my life, young one," he said, wiping away a tear.

"It's nothing, sir. These women have offered me a lot of fruits. I think that evens us out," he grinned.

The chief let out a light-hearted laugh. The boy noticed that the chief was a pretty big person and even at this age, he was a lot stronger than him – at least he looked like he was. All these years of hard, mountain life and hunting had given him a lot of scars. If he were any skinnier or his hair was longer, like, a lot longer, he'd be just like his father.

"Come on in, dear boy."

He guided the boy to their hut.

"No worries, people. The Yaazhi is no threat. Just please leave it alone. And please do not provoke it. Also, we will have a campfire tonight, a special one, to receive our special guest – the man who saved the women of our village. I personally invite everybody in the village to be there at the gathering," he announced assuringly to the people, who were standing in groups, obviously terrified by the animal. The children were giggling while their parents pulled them closer so they wouldn't run up to the Yaazhi.

"Oh no, Ayya. Please do not trouble your people," the boy protested as he walked into the chief's abode. He felt very different as he stepped into the place. For a moment, he forgot that he had travelled a thousand miles. For a brief moment, it felt like he hadn't left home after all. For that one small fragment in time, he felt like he was home. It even smelled a lot like his place. He was brought back to his senses by Nambirajan's deep voice.

"No, son. You do not understand."

The chief put his hand on the boy's shoulder and walked him a little further into his home, taking him into a room. In the room, hung a huge skull; almost as big as the boy himself. With two huge tusks, as big as his arm span, he immediately recognized what it was.

"Wow, you people killed one?"

"Not me, unfortunately no. Valli, get the boy some water, will you? And bring him something to eat, as well."

Valli expected the boy to refuse food since he'd just had a lot of mangoes. But he just kept staring at the skull.

"May I touch it?" he asked, his expression a lot more sincere now. All the playfulness was gone. The chief nodded. His fingers first traced the fist-sized hole on the forehead of the now-dead Yaazhi.

"Yaazhis are, how do you put it, they're creatures from a different world. Or at least it's believed so. There aren't more than a handful throughout this mountain and the ranges around us. No outsider has seen any like them, and we believe they're exclusive to this land. They live for a thousand years or more. We, the people who have been living here, have never seen one more than three or four times. Throughout our history, Yaazhis have only made us aware of their presence, and we've never got closer to one, except for this one," he explained, pointing to the hanging skull. "They're territorial, vegetarian, calm, humongous, kind, and monstrous. They have an extensive way of communicating, just not in words. We aren't sure what it is, but there's always a web around them. An invisible web around their herd. They're unique, and no one except for my great-great-grandfather got the chance to touch one. Miserable that he had to kill one to do it. This one, just like the one outside, was in its musth when it started rampaging our then settlement. Without a herd, they run into musth cycles very frequently. My ancestor was the one who killed it, single-handedly. When he saw his people being killed, huts being flattened, and everything that we'd built until then collapse because of this one enormous God-sent monstrosity, he picked up that piece of teak wood," he pointed to a very old yet intact piece of wood kept in the corner of the room, "and ran up the Yaazhi's legs. He stood on top of it and drove the wood through the Yaazhi's armour-thick skin. Being able to save people from a Yaazhi, a raging one, is not a simple thing, son. Nor is Yaazhi a simple wild animal. They're beings bound by something far more eternal, something other than just hunger and sex like all other beings." He turned towards the boy, looked him straight in the eye, and continued, "That's how we became the clan that we are, son. We're God-men because of him. The settlement of Kurinji would've been long-lost if not for the great warrior that my great-great-grandfather was, and it would've lost most of its female population if not for you. You are as important to our village as the founders of this settlement," he said, pure gratefulness in his eyes. The boy turned towards the teak spear and took his own spear out. He placed the stone edge pointing to the wood, knelt and prayed to it to give him the strength. The strength to be able to put one's life on the line for others. The room's vibe was getting to him, and he felt too overwhelmed by everything he'd seen. He walked out of the abode and Valli brought him a pot full of water and a few pieces of jackfruit dipped in honey. He took them, thanked her, and walked out to sit near the Yaazhi. He hadn't noticed it until then, but the animal was still standing there, in the same place he'd left it. He put his hand forth, and the animal, in an awe-inducing manner, dropped to his knees and sat down next to him. He sang a little, a very familiar song that his father always sang to the animals in his colony.

"Damn, this jackfruit honey combination is wildly intoxicating," he said mid-song, and the Yaazhi lifted its head as though it wanted him to just shut up and sing, and he did just that. The water, which he assumed should be from the mountain springs, tasted the sweetest, like the one from the glaciers up in his home. He wondered why this place brought back so many memories, but he slowly let go of that thought. He simply lost himself in the songs that he was singing, and the fruits he was eating.

Chapter 03
Fire and Dance

The evening that came brought with it a very different feeling. The chief brought him a garland, made mainly of little white and senkanthal flowers, and gave him a warm hug. He then proudly described to everyone gathered around the campfire about everything the boy had done for the people of the village. The boy was secretly thankful that it was a little dark and that the people could not see him clearly, even though there was a huge fire burning in the middle of the gathering. This was the first time he had been invited to one of these gatherings. He'd seen a couple of these bonfires happening in a few different villages that he'd earlier crossed, but they usually only allowed the people of the village to attend.

The crowd was asked not to cheer too much so as to not agitate the Yaazhi, which was still on the brink of their settlement. Despite that, the women the boy had saved, who were a part of the gathering party along with their families, could not resist cheering in sheer joy. He simply stood there, awkwardly. He understood that this was a big deal for them, but to him, he had simply used a little trick that his father used on animals to calm them down when they were agitated. This was all too much. He simply bowed, taking their greetings.

"Ayya, who are you?" a child in the front asked.

"Uncle, what is your name?"

"Where are you from?"

A lot of questions popped up from the crowd. He realized he had to speak.

"Well, I come from a similar culture, one that hails from the pahadis, I mean, the mountains. I come from a very faraway place, filled with snow. My father, just like ayya here, was the chief of our campsite. I left home to travel when I was very young, maybe when I was like you," he explained, pointing to a young eleven or twelve-year-old boy in the crowd. "Ever since, I've been travelling and climbing mountains. I do not intend to go anywhere in particular, but I must say, I am thankful I started travelling back when I did. As a result, I met you people and everything else that happened after," he smiled.

He was genuine about this one. He was thankful for the life he had now, although he missed his family terribly. More so, at that exact moment. His father would be proud. He saw Valli standing there, still occasionally looking at the Yaazhi, which was now asleep. For a brief moment, they locked eyes and he was the one to look away first from her piercing glare.

The village then went on to celebrate the occasion with a bit of drink for everyone, the one they called Kal. Women had something different called Naravu, and the children were sent to play around a smaller campfire, laid at a watching distance from the primary one. The boy was given a drink as well, and he had had such pleasures only a few times before. Nonetheless, he had picked a habit of his own, one he caught on to from the land he hailed from. With the permission of the chief, he went to their abode, picked up a little pouch from his bag, and opened it. There were clear instructions from his father on how to use them. So, he carried it very carefully to the campfire and sat down with folded legs. He loaded the stone chillum he'd made a few years ago with the bhangh leaves that he'd crushed up. He looked up, raised his chillum, and noticed that the people around him grew quiet. He closed his eyes, and prayed to the heavens, thanking it for the pleasure that life had given him.

"Ohm rudraaya namaha," he muttered under his breath and picked up a burning twig from the fire. He took a deep drag, and let out a big cloud of smoke. The elderly around him were familiar with what he had and smiled. The chief signalled one of his men to bring out their pipes, and the campfire quickly turned into a smoking circle.

"Son, how did you know about this..." the chief paused as though he was searching for the right words, "habit?"

There was little sound except for the crackling fire. The women were now retiring to their huts while Valli and a few others sat around at the other end of the fire.

"My father gave it to me when I left for my voyage and asked me not to treat this as an intoxicant, but as a medicine and a refuge. A place to go to, only when you need guidance or feel like you need to savour the moment. I thought I had to savour this campfire with you folks, and so," he smiled and showed his chillum.

"We feel the same way about you, ayya," an elder replied. The boy knew the word 'ayya' was used to address the elderly and respected people. He was not comfortable being either of them to an elder.

"You can call me by my name, ayya. I am a small man compared to all of you who take responsibility for an entire settlement. My family called me Karthik."

He could not remember the last time he said his name to someone else. He'd never had to.

"Karthikeya, you deserve more than just our respect. You deserve a place in our prayers, for generations to come. You have saved our women, which means, you have saved our lineage. Lose a man, you lose a soldier. Lose a woman, you lose a potential bloodline. We have many soldiers, son. But we only have one bloodline, the one of our Kurinji. You've saved our Kurinji women, and we thank you for that."

The elder raised his wooden pipe. All other men, who were taking tokes and drinking, raised their pipes and coconut shells in unison. Karthik bowed out of pure respect. Nobody could tell because it was now midnight, but Karthik knew he was tearing up.

"What did you do to stop the Yaazhi, Karthikeya, if I may?" Valli asked, from across the fire. Her smooth skin bounced off the light from the fire as did the moon.

"I sang," he smiled.

"Do you people sing?" he asked, turning around the men.

"We sing, dance, carve, and occasionally even paint the nearby caves. But how does singing calm a raging animal?" Chief Nambi was genuinely curious.

"My father taught me that singing, dancing, and other art forms were not merely for entertainment. Just like this," he pointed to his chillum. "He said that art or anything that arises out of a higher calling, other than a physical need, serves a harmonic purpose. A certain tune stills the mind, a certain one stirs it, a certain one brings rage, while another brings calm. He specifically taught one that brings pained, overwhelmed minds to ease. The Yaazhi was simply too enraged and out of control. There was a metal knife stuck to its front left foot. I pulled it out, and the animal was still raging. So, I sang, and it calmed down," he said as though this wasn't really a matter of discussion at all. But that didn't stop the fascination of the people around.

"Can you sing it for us? A lot of us are still pretty stressed," a woman near Valli said, and the women around laughed. He turned a little red from embarrassment but was okay doing it. In fact, he felt like singing and dancing as well.

"Only if you promise to dance, amma," he said.

"Oh, sure. Valli and I are the best dancers in the village."

She pulled Valli up. Valli swayed a little before she stood still and positioned herself.

"Ayya, do we have your permission?" she asked chief Nambi. He was always a proud father who liked to see his self-taught daughter dance. He nodded, and the women squatted down to touch the ground. They said their prayers before they readied themselves. Karthik closed his eyes, thought of a good song to go with this village's beautiful vibe, and started singing.

He'd never sung for so many people before, ever. So, he had to be a little louder. He sang about the mountains and the clear water, the chilled breeze, and the successful hunt that they'd had – a song his mother sang every time their folks finished a hunt. It seemed to fit the people of Kurinji too. Valli and the woman weren't synchronized, but they moved in harmony, letting the song take control of them. Karthik, mesmerized by the fire, the breeze, and the pure love the people there gave him, sang his heart out, his voice reaching everyone around the fire. Everybody swayed a little, tapping hands in unison, and it wasn't long before a couple of other women joined Valli and her partner. After a beautiful song, Karthik came to a stop, landing the song smoothly. The people came down as if they were feathers carried by the wind to the ground. As soon as he finished, an elder started singing, and then Valli, and then a few more people sang. They continued dancing, and it wasn't until dawn broke that they realized how much time had passed.

"Karthikeya," Nambi said as he stood up, swaying from the drinks and the bhangh, "your father has taught you well. I pray that he lives a long, healthy life, and so does your entire family."

"I do too," Karthik smiled. He liked that the people had changed his name a little. The Yaazhi was still there, now awake. It was eating from the nearby shrubs. '*Guess it couldn't care to stand up,*' he thought. He refused the chief's offer to rest in their abode and simply asked for someone to hand him his bag so he could sleep outside. Valli gave him the bag and thanked him once again for everything.

"Your song," she started. "I've never danced so spontaneously before. You should teach me how to sing that openly," she said.

The dim light of dawn made her seem a little darker, yet impeccably beautiful. Karthik agreed to teach her some time, and in return asked to watch her dance in daylight. When asked where he was going to sleep, he simply pointed to the Yaazhi and said, "On top of my friend," and grinned. She could not take him seriously nor could she take him for a goof. When Karthik finally set up his makeshift bed and lay down, he heard a distant rooster cry. When the children walked out of the huts in the morning, they wondered why their parents were still asleep, and why the man from the last night's campfire was sleeping on top of a Yaazhi that was casually munching on shrubs.

Chapter 04
The Sadhu Caves

Karthik woke up around noon, just alongside half the village. Valli was watering the flower plants near her hut and greeted him with folded hands. He returned the greeting and walked over to a little mountain spring to wash himself up a little before returning to the camp. '*I should pick some honey up*,' he thought. '*The honey and jackfruit combination was heavenly yesterday.*' He also wanted to look for bhang plants on the way, in case he'd used all his stock the previous night. He didn't remember how much he had smoked or drank. He remembered two things from last night – chief Nambi's tear-filled thanks and Valli's beautiful dance. Valli had told him that his song made her dance. He alone knew that her silhouette and the campfire had shaped his song's tune.

The chief's abode was all cleaned up, and two banana leaves were placed on the ground as he walked into there.

"Sit, Karthikeya. Time to taste a proper Kurinji meal this time," chief Nambi said. His voice had such a powerful base to it.

"The hunting party returned?" Karthik asked, his face a little disappointed. He'd hoped to join the party last minute and hunt some small game for his way forward. The wolf meat would've gone bad anyway. He never got time to heat it. He didn't want to do it in a campfire, he knew the people took offence to cook in a campfire gathering.

"Yes, and this time, after a long year, we've got a lot of gazelles and some wild chickens. Should get us through the next ten, fifteen days."

"How do you make meat last that long?"

"We cut it all up into smaller strips or pieces, sprinkle a little citrus, dry it out in the sun, and keep it all in our attic. The attic is kept cool and completely dry at all times. We also store food categorized by their shelf life, so that one spoilt item does not spoil the rest of the lot," Valli explained as she sat down to serve the food.

"Have you eaten?" Karthik asked Valli and her mother.

"Yes, long back. Unlike some people, we do not sleep until the sun hits our bum," Valli's mother complained and brought in the boiled sweet potatoes.

"I was wondering if I could take some honey with me today. Or please tell me if I can exchange the honey for some other meat. I can go hunt a small game in exchange for some honey," Karthik said as he gobbled a hot piece of the sweet potato. "I am really craving some honey and jackfruit. What you gave me that day was delicious," he said to Valli.

"Wait, let me get you some to eat now," Valli stood up, and walked up to their attic. "Do you want to try having some bananas mixed with it as well? Goes really well with the honey and jackfruit," she suggested, standing on the stairs. She was excited that someone finally liked her favourite snack.

Karthik did not want to spoil the recipe but agreed anyway. He was, however, going to get some honey, or at least he assumed he was. He could then make the snack whenever he wanted. He just had to find a jackfruit tree, which was in plenty around the settlement.

"Can you bring a couple of extra bananas? For my friend outside," he beamed.

"You're sure a couple would be enough for that big of a friend?"

"Well, he's loading up on the shrubs near him anyway. I'm just asking for some so I can feed him myself."

"Okay," she shouted, disappearing into the attic.

The chief was not amused.

"Are you planning to leave today?" he asked, frowning a little.

"Well, yes," Karthik replied. He rarely stayed in settlements, and even if he did, it was never more than a day.

"Why? Do you have some place to be?"

"Um. No."

"Then what's the hurry? Spend a few more days with us, we have a very special day coming up."

"What day?"

"The sun festival," Valli exclaimed, running down the stairs. She dropped the bananas on the ground. "Hehe, sorry. But yea, the sun festival."

"The what?"

"God, are you deaf? Sun, sun. Big yellow ball in the sky, sun," Valli said, picking the bananas up. "Here, feed your friend. People from all the mountain areas gather around once a year. We bring plants and produce from our settlements, and celebrate the sun festival. It's our way of thanking nature and the sun for being the source of our prosperity."

She continued placing sweet potatoes on Karthik's leaf.

"I think that's enough for me," Karthik said, putting his hand out to stop her after the third one. He'd already eaten a couple.

"Shu, eat one with honey and millet flour. This is my special recipe. I hope you like it," she gave him a death stare. "Anyway, the festival begins with..."

"Hello, leave the boy alone. Let him eat in peace. Yapping, yapping, yapping and yapping all day long. We should've named you Palli instead because you keep yapping all day with no attempt at being productive," Valli's mother said and took her outside the abode.

"The festival sounds interesting, but unfortunately, I am not really a stay-at-one-place kind of guy," Karthik frowned.

He'd never heard of the sun festival before. The one celebration back home was to welcome summer as their winters were long and unforgiving. Therefore, their village along with a couple of other floating settlements came together on the penultimate night of the winter and shared stories of that particular winter. He'd never been to a festival of any sort since he left home.

"You will only have to stay for a week or so," chief Nambi said, hoping the boy would stay. He wanted to show the boy off to the other villages too. He wanted to show the Yaazhi off as well. "You can actually stay in the caves nearby if you aren't comfortable living in the village. The caves are where we used to live. That's where we usually let the travellers stay if they ever want a place to crash. It's a two-minute walk from here, and there is a spring near it. We will bring you food up there."

He did like the idea of a cave. He agreed to stay for a week. Valli and a couple of other women were asked to clean the cave up and set the bed. He politely refused and said that he had a bed of his own, and could take care of himself. Valli alone accompanied to show him where the cave was, and the Yaazhi was already following the two of them. Valli turned around often, a little less nervous now that she'd seen it do no harm for over two days. Still, the sheer presence of it made her anxious.

"Relax, he's not gonna do anything."

"Well, he was inches away from trampling me into a pool of blood and guts. Don't blame me for being a little nervous, good sir."

"Good point."

"Where's the knife thing?" she asked.

"In here," he replied, tapping on the bag over his shoulders.

"What is this?" Valli asked, pointing to the glider.

"You saw me use it, didn't you? It's a glider. We use it to come downhill. My father built it. It's a makeshift bed too, a part-time shield, and a full-time glider," he explained as he picked up a bunch of gooseberries.

"Eww, gooseberries," Valli made a face. "They're just so bitter."

"You honestly don't know, do you?"

"Yea, yea I know. Water tastes better after. But I would rather eat something sweet to start with, and continue to eat sweets."

"You have a sweet tooth problem."

They reached the caves. There were a few openings, all of them reaching far inside the hills. One of them was a little small, relatively, and reached into the mountain just enough to provide shelter.

"We used to come here all the time, me and my friends. There were also a few sadhus here, always brooding and doing all kinds of prayers. Then our parents asked us not to come here and make a ruckus because it would disturb the sadhus. We gradually stopped. The sadhus are nowhere to be seen these days. Maybe they all died. Pretty old people, you know. Big beards with one cute bun on the top of their heads. Some weird-looking people they are," she made face gestures as though she was tracing a long beard and bun.

"Sadhus are weird people," Karthik sighed, tossing a gooseberry seed into the void. He heard the clear water spring nearby. He wanted to drink some water. Even normal water tasted sweet after gooseberries, imagine how the water from here would taste?

"Our people called them babas, and the people in the desserts called them yogis. But the one thing they have in common is that they all look bizarre. You know, I once saw one of them wearing human bones for a necklace. And there was another who wore the skull of a deer, with the antelope and all, as a headpiece. He looked ridiculous, you know. Like a moose."

He put his hands on his head as though they were horns and strutted around. Valli laughed.

"Where all have you been?" she asked curiously.

"A lot of places. I was born on a snowy mountain," he flinched a little as soon as he realized he said born, but continued anyway. The poor girl didn't have to know a lot about him. "But I quickly grew tired and bored of the place. My father offered me a chance to explore the world, and so I started my journey. Since then, I have travelled south. There are mighty rivers, huge forests, vast deserts, plains, and countless small hills like this one."

"Small? This is the highest peak around here, okay," Valli got all defensive.

"From where I come, this is called a pebble," he laughed.

"Shu, leave our mountain alone."

She threw a pebble at him. He sat down near the spring and took a sip of the water.

"Ah, this is heavenly."

The Yaazhi slowly walked up to the spring and had some water. After a while, it just sat near the water spring and decided it was a good shady place for a quick nap. These two didn't look like they would stop speaking anytime soon anyway. In a few minutes, the Yaazhi had fallen asleep, and the cave was ready to be occupied.

Chapter 05

Painting a Destiny

That evening was a lazy one for Karthik. He was given a torch to find his way around after sunset, and Valli had brought his dinner an hour ago. He had just fed the Yaazhi some fruits; not that he needed to. It was fine on its own. He did notice that the animal was unnaturally calm, yet felt its presence around him all the time. The caves always emitted a weird hum. He had grown up with caves humming around him, so this wasn't new to him. In fact, the hum invoked a very familiar feeling in him. He had, in all these years, due to travel and tiredness, disconnected himself from what he really loved as a young child – art. He used to sing, dance, paint, and even sculpt with his father and mother. He was yet to see a woman dance with as much aggression as his mother, and a man sing with as much throw as his father.

He had a sudden burst of inspiration and began searching for flowers. He walked around, picked flowers in colours that he liked, and came back to his cave to prepare the dyes. These wouldn't last as long in the cave, but he couldn't care less. He simply wanted to paint, for now. The roots and hair from the wolf hide made for good brushes.

He now had all that he needed – a few colours, some brushes, and lots of rocks to paint on. Now, he just needed to think of what to paint. He wondered if the sadhus were still around in the nearby cave. He liked painting in deeper caves, where there was rarely any sunlight. His father always said that paintings lasted a little longer when they stayed out of the sunlight since it changed the complexion of the colours. He took his torch and began wandering inside the caves. As he walked into the caves, their hum, their smell, the complete silence of the caves, the stark darkness, except for the fire torch he had, all of it made it a memory he knew he was going to carry for the rest of his life.

Finally, he found a large clearing inside of one of the caves and decided it was a good place to paint. He set the torch down into one of the cracks and started painting. He never really painted with a particular image in his head. He liked starting out with a simple idea and expanding on it as he painted.

He did the same here. First, there was a campfire. A bright, shimmering campfire. With people around it. And then, there was a woman. A woman with dark skin. She was dancing, her arms and legs resembling the flares of the fire itself. When he was done with the painting, he took a step back and saw it in its full glory. He had painted Valli. He laughed a little at how he had left the face empty, with no features.

"Do you not know how to paint faces?" a voice asked. He was taken aback by the sheer suddenness of the voice. He looked around to find a short man with a long beard and man-bun sitting near the torch he had placed, eating gooseberries. "Or is that an artistic choice?"

"Ayya."

He knew the man was a sadhu. He touched the man's feet and got back on his own.

"May you live a long life, and may the world become a better place with you in it," the sadhu smiled. "You never answered my question."

"I'm afraid I have never been able to capture the beauty of a human face, especially eyes, in any of my paintings. So, after a couple of failed attempts, I left my paintings as they were, with no facial features."

"So you don't know how to paint faces? I see. However, I think it makes for a great artistic choice as well. Faceless figures. Their expressions are left open for comprehension."

The sadhu stood up and took a step forward towards Karthik. He was only as tall as Karthik's chest, so he had to look up to meet his glance. "Karthikeya, you have decided to arrive, finally," he said, with a feeling alien to Karthik.

"I do not remember introducing myself to you," Karthik replied in bewilderment. Was he one of the people gathered around the campfire?

"Oh, neither did I introduce myself. How rude, sorry. My name is Agathiyan. Welcome to this creepy little fellow's humble abode. Don't mind the bats, though. I keep them for the occasional fruits they bring in for me," he laughed and started walking. "Come with me," he called Karthik.

Karthik made sure the knife he had picked up from the Yaazhi was still with him, as all of this was making him uncomfortable. He wasn't going to follow a stranger into what looked like a void of a cave.

"Don't worry, you won't be needing a knife to kill an old dwarf," the sadhu turned around and smiled. What in the world is happening here? Karthik ran behind the sadhu to keep up with him.

"We are the muni folk, you see. I am the only one here though. The rest are, well, I don't know where they are. But I am sure they're doing very fine," the man kept talking, but Karthik had to interrupt.

"I'm sorry, ayya, but were you at the campfire yesterday?" How did he know his name?

"Well, where am I not there? Do you know? It's not really by choice that I was there at your campfire, or at the time of your birth or your parents' wedding ceremony. Oh, how afraid I was that I'd miss your parents' wedding. Your father is a very great man for letting me see him and your mother in their entire glory as a newly-wedded couple. I'd have been crazy mad at him had he not shown up here in his marriage outfit, you know? I'd have bickered about it through eternity. Good for him, good for him. They're doing pretty well, in case you're wondering how your parents are doing, and so is everybody back home. I mean, back at your home," he continued.

What the hell is this man going on about? What the absolute hell?

"Their marriage?" Karthik exclaimed. "You were at their marriage? Wait, who are you?"

"Well, did you not hear me? I'm Agathian. Keep up, kid. I have a lot to tell, and if you are going to ask me everything twice, I think you'll be stuck here for a very long time. And no, I wasn't at their wedding. They asked me not to come. Somebody had to be here and not there, and all others bailed on me. I was stuck here because your father was more of a righteous man than a friend. He came here after his marriage so I'd not be mad at him for not being able to see him on the day of his marriage. Oh, how beautiful they looked together! How absolutely beautiful he and your mother looked in their marriage costumes. Good man, good man. Your father, you know? Real good man, but an absolutely bad friend, he dared to have a marriage without me. Well, good for him, at least I was there to save him from the absolute imbalance his marriage had caused in this world," he laughed.

"I do not understand anything." Karthik stopped walking. He was wondering if he should simply walk away because there was no way his parents had been here before.

"Well, you don't really have to, you know. I'm here to tell you about what is ahead of you, not what's behind you. Or me. What's past is past, and you have to know only what you need to. But I'm not here to tell you about your past. No, no I'm not. I'm here because you've finally come to meet this old uncle, and uncle has been waiting for years to simply show you something and continue my journey down south. I have been waiting, you know."

Karthik was now convinced that this man was a little loose up in his head, but still didn't know how he knew his name. Maybe he was at the campfire after all.

"Hold this, will you?" He returned Karthik's torch.

The sadhu then squeezed himself into a narrow path and crossed it. "Come on now, don't be shy. Walk in here," he called out from the other side.

"No, ayya. I'm good, I think. I have to leave now," Karthik replied, thinking to himself that the sadhu had gone a little off-balance in the brain after years of isolation. Is this what would happen to him if he stayed alone for too long? He shook his head.

"Leave? And go where, young Karthikeya? You do not have any other work, anyway," the sadhu laughed.

His voice echoed a little, and Karthik figured that he was standing inside a similar clearing on the other side of the rock.

"Come on in, you showed me a painting, now it's my turn to show you one."

Karthik sighed and crossed the narrow path. When he entered the other side, he found himself in a dome-shaped clearing, with only one way to get in and out – the one he and the sadhu had come through.

"So, welcome to my home," the muni exclaimed. Karthik noticed a lingam in the centre of the dome. He'd never seen one anywhere but his father's cave.

"That..." Karthik pointed and started speaking.

"Yea, yea, yea. But that's not what I wanted to show you. Here, take a look at the walls." The muni handed him the torch and sat himself down on a leaf bed on one side of the hall. "Now, I'm not the one who drew it, alright? I'm a humble restorer, who made a few strokes here and there, whenever the dye became a little lighter or the rocks chipped off in some places."

Karthik walked nearer to the walls, where there was a painting of a peacock. "A peacock?"

"Well, if you really care about continuity, I suggest you start near the entrance," the muni replied, still munching on fruits. Karthik felt like he was walking on a smooth, silky hide. The sadhu must've laid them throughout. He walked towards the entrance and found the beginning of the painting.

There was a huge mountain covered with snow. As he walked along the walls, he saw paintings of a child, alone at a lake. Then the child grew up to be a boy, alongside a man and a woman, blue and green. He traced the walls a little more to find a man walking alone in the woods. Then, the man was flying on a peacock, and riding a large, black animal. It could be a Yaazhi, given its sheer size in comparison to the man. The paintings went on to show the man's life, and it didn't take a long time before Karthik turned around to the sadhu, and said, "This, this is me."

"Well, yea. Why would I invite you in here then? I really like the colour of the peacock, do you?"

He did. The peacock. He remembered how he and his father had carefully mixed together a bunch of colours to bring that shade for his glider.

"But, how?" What was happening here, again? "Who are you, ayya?"

"What? Boy, how many times do I tell you? I'm Agathian. Now come over here, don't stress yourself out too much. Have a gooseberry."

Karthik sat down near him.

"Look Karthikeya, I've been here for a very long time. I've grown a little older, but none wiser. I don't know a lot of things myself, you know. I only know how to chant the name of Rudra, and that of your father's, and meditate upon it. But if you have questions, ask away, and let's see if I know the answers to them. But I'm also a little sleepy, so you'll have to make it quick. I really do not want to sleep next to you, no offence. My body is too old to take kicks and flips."

"First question, how do you know I kick in my sleep?" Karthik glared.

"Well, I see that the no offence warning did not really work."

"Fine, who made the painting?"

"I do not know. Neither did any of my friends, honestly. Collectively, we all know a lot of things, so this missing information is a mystery. We have a very wild guess, but there's no solid evidence. You see, I know a few things about your past, because well, the past has already happened, and everybody has access to that information. So, I know about your life in the mountains and your thirst for knowledge, and the questions you asked your father as well as his answers and requests. He is a great man, that he is, but he has a very weird way of giving answers to the very simple questions you ask him. We suspect that this," the muni fanned his arms, showing the wall, "is a little clue for you to find the answers to the questions you have in mind. Of course, you can choose to really avoid all this and simply go do your own thing, you know. We're curious about it too, but I highly doubt you'll be able to simply stand there and watch everything burn. It's your destiny, after all, you know," the sadhu once again seemed to speak incoherently, caught up in his own train of thoughts.

"Ayya," Karthik stopped the sadhu and decided to give structure to this mess. "If you didn't know who painted this, how did you know it was about me? Also, what's with all the destiny talk? What is going on here? I'm just a nomad, born to a simple village chief and a loving mother."

"Lies, lies, all of it I say. Is denying what you are something you were born with, or did you pick it up as part of your stupid journey? Your father is not simply a village chief, your parents aren't really your parents, and you, you are anything but just a nomad. However, I get it. When you live long enough with lies, they become your truth. But understand this, they're just your truths, and you are simply a reflection of what you believe. So, stop putting yourself in a circle of denial, child, and start believing in all the things that you once questioned."

"How do you know all this?"

"Damn it, child. Listen. I bring you to see the picture, and you ask me who drew it. I tell you the truth, and you ask the nature of my existence. Why do you ponder on triviality when presented with something the entire mankind is looking for?"

"And what is it looking for?" Finally, the sadhu was getting somewhere.

"A purpose, son. Your purpose, unlike the rest of us, is defined," the sadhu showed him the walls again.

"What if I want to be a simple nomad?"

"Ah, that is an interesting question. We don't know. You've always been a mystery to us, and quite frankly, even to your father. And trust me when I say this, he isn't easily amused by a lot of things. The man is quite present, you know, but never really. He didn't expect you to leave, first things first. And now this, so you'll always find a way to amaze your father, but the question is, at what cost?"

"I don't see any cost."

"That's because you don't know what's coming after the people. What's coming, or to be frank, what's already here and expanding, Karthikeya, is a tumour on the land. It and you, are moving closer to each other, every day. What happens when you two meet is what we're really unsure of. The weight of fate is not to be fiddled with this callously. But that's what always happens, doesn't it? The people of that village, the people around the land you're about to go to, and if left unchecked, the people of all the lands that you've crossed, all of them will suffer."

"Suffer? Because I choose to be a nomad? How? What's coming? What does any of this have to do with me?"

"The ghosts, son. The ghosts are coming. No, not the normal ones. These ghosts aren't dead, no. They're very alive. These ghosts are filled with greed, and when they happen to cross paths with the people you've just met, the settlement you just visited, just like everything else on their path, will perish. The people will suffer, and the land will fall prey to a curse. The ghosts, are coming."

The muni took the torch and touched a part of the wall with the fire. In the light, Karthik saw a painting of a large group of people. Big, big people with clubs and sticks and other shimmering weapons. He saw an army.

"That…" he hesitated.

"That is the destiny you failed to serve once. That is destiny coming for you. The last time, it came for you. This time, we assume it's coming for a lot of us."

"I don't…"

"Yes, you don't. I don't expect you to. To be fair, even we can only comprehend what's happening. The why, well, we can comprehend the what because we don't question the why, but even if we attempt to question it, we wouldn't understand it. Don't question the things that happen for a reason, son. Instead, question your part in the happening."

"My part? What does an army have to do with me?"

"That is a question for you, not me. Now, if you'll excuse me, I am going to sleep. You can look at the pictures for as long as you want, but remember, sleep outside. Or, if you're going to take too long, I will sleep outside." The sadhu paused and continued, "You know what, I'm too old for the cold too. Also, I cannot sleep on the hard floor, hence the animal hide on the floor. Do you happen to have an animal hide of some kind that I can use?"

"No, no, ayya. You can sleep here. I am not sure I can sleep anyway, with all this…" What the hell is this? "… information," he sighed. "I will just take one more good look at all that's here, and go back outside to sleep."

"Good, good. Kind man you are, just like your father. He would sleep on hard ice with nothing at all to protect him. I can't do that. You know what, I think he shouldn't do that either. Why go out of your way to struggle and remain that nonchalant? What's left for him to prove and to whom is he proving it anyway?"

'*This man really loved getting lost in his own thoughts,*' Karthik thought.

"Ayya," Karthik interrupted again. "If I may, just one last question?"

"Yea, yea, yea. Go ahead."

"How does my father know you?"

The muni laughed, a very hearty laugh. It echoed through the cave and finally, he began, "Whom or what does he not know, Karthikeya? The real question is, how do I know of him? I know him as my teacher, mentor, friend, and guide. For that, I am fortunate."

The muni closed his eyes, and joined his hands together, raising them above his head. "For that, I am very fortunate."

In the little light that the torch provided, Karthik saw a teardrop roll down the sadhu's cheeks.

For who knows how long, Karthik just stood near the walls with the torch. In some time, the torch went out and he had to go outside with literally no light at all. Good thing he remembered his way out. He did fall down a couple of times, but then thought, '*What's an adventure without some scathing and blood?*' That night he didn't sleep. He simply sat there, staring at the stars and the night. The Yaazhi would move now and then. He wasn't sure if he really wanted to stay for the sun festival anymore. He just had to see Valli one last time before he left this place. If the Yaazhi came, he'd take it with him through his journey. If not, it was back to square one, just him roaming around in the woods.

Chapter 06

The Waterfall

The next day, Karthik woke up as soon as he heard something move near him. He then realized it was just the Yaazhi, and sighed in relief. The Yaazhi was unamused by his sudden movements. It stopped eating for a brief second, then went back to its munching again.

"Do you ever get tired of eating, my friend?" Karthik punched the Yaazhi's legs, and it spun around a little so that the tail came and hit Karthik on his face. "Woah, we're throwing hands now? Come on, show me whatchu got?" he feigned to sprawl.

The Yaazhi simply continued eating, dropping one of the little twigs on his head, and moved to the next tree. "You know what, I'll leave you because you got me a neem twig."

Karthik started brushing his teeth with the twig. He walked inside the sadhu's cave with the twig still in his mouth, and this time he decided not to question how or why. He only wanted to know the 'what'. When he got to the first clearing, he saw the painting he had made yesterday. It seemed so beautiful in the little daylight that reached there. As he continued into the cave, the light dimmed a lot more. By the time he reached the sadhu's narrow cave entrance, there was almost no light. He crossed the entrance, and to his surprise, the other side was very bright. He looked up to find that the cave's dome had a very small crack at the top, which lit the entire place up. The light from the crack fell directly on the lingam, and he knelt down before it to say his prayers. There was no sign of the sadhu, but the painting seemed a lot more vibrant than he'd remembered from the previous night.

As he saw the paintings on the wall around him, part after part, they unfolded like a story. Up until the Yaazhi's part, he recognized his life, and after that, he simply observed. He walked to the very beginning of the painting, near the entrance of the dome. The lake. His mother had shown him the lake when he was six years old. The lake, where they had found him as a baby. And then the mountains, the mountains where he grew up. His father, his mother, him. Looking at it, it seemed as though he'd re-lived his life. He then moved to the other side of the dome, the part after the Yaazhi. The part with the army. Most of it was covered in blue ink. '*The Sadhu is not a very good restorer,*' he thought. There were a lot of things he didn't understand. Structures he didn't recognize, symbols that didn't make sense, and a lot more. Most of the part after the Yaazhi was a huge blob of colours like blue, yellow, brown, and orange. Orange was mainly the fires. That much he understood. Fires that burnt a lot of people. Why wouldn't he understand that? It was all he knew, and most of the conversations he'd had with his father, had been at the cremation ground.

He remembered the day his father had asked him to join the guardians of the village. To fend off the constant waves of intruders and wild beasts that kept attacking the village for it was on the better side of the forest, with access to what little water and other resources the gruesome mountains had to offer. He remembered how he was afraid to do the same thing that his father often did. Burn the bodies of the casualties of war, from both their village and the pillagers. Day after day, every day. He recollected not wanting to take up the role of the village's guardian and remembered talking to his father. He remembered everything, clear as it happened just then.

"I am not a war monger, pa. I despise fights, I despise killing, and I value life over everything. Our settlement, our personal benefit, the river, everything. Life is far too valuable to be taken for a piece of land. I can kill to eat, fine. But I am not killing in the name of another life."

"And that is why I think you would be a good guardian."

"I don't think my spear has the will to kill a man, even if it is to protect another."

"Will comes from the heart, my darling son, not from a stone spear."

"I do not want to do this, father," I refused, one last time.

"So be it," he smiled and closed his eyes to meditate. His father always recited hymns in front of the bodies. He apologized for the gruelling life they'd had and promised to not kill them again. He believed that the dead we pray for will protect us from the living. He didn't understand the hypocrisy nor did he like killing. Father or not, Karthik didn't like hypocrisy. He decided to leave the settlement that was under a man he didn't entirely agree with.

That night, Karthik left his village to travel down south, in search of nothing in particular. His mother had fondly given him a little advice and a new spear in exchange for his blunt one; his father had still not opened his eyes. As he left, he turned to his father sitting in a trance. With his eyes still closed, he simply raised his right arm as though he had blessed him just then, and from a distance, Karthik bowed down to touch the ground. How he was as a chief, he didn't care. How he was as a father, he very much did. He regretted every step he took away from his loving father. Once over the clearing, he stood on the edge of a cliff. He turned to his village one last time, took a deep breath, and dived off the cliff.

Inside the cave, he searched some more for the sadhu, but couldn't find him anywhere. He came out of the cave, packed his stuff into the bag, and waited for Valli to turn up. In the meanwhile, he decided it was a good time to wash the Yaazhi's wound and apply some fresh mud again. He started cleaning it up.

"Giving your friend a bath?" he heard Valli behind him after some time.

"Ah, Valli. Good morning!" he wished. "And no, just giving his wound a little dressing. The mud, if stays without replacement for too long could worsen a wound and..."

"We know, okay. We know. Come eat," she scoffed.

Karthik finished and sat down near Valli. She served him some jackfruit, millet powder, a few mangoes and offered him a coconut shell with honey. "Thank you for the food, I appreciate it."

"Thank you for saving our lives."

"Wow, how many times, huh? I am beginning to grow so tired of your gratefulness that I wish I had let my friend here trample you," Karthik said as he took out a piece of jackfruit, dipped it in honey, and ate it.

"Eh, lazy you. Wait, let me mix it all up, then eat." Valli mixed everything up, took a handful, and ate it. "Mmm, see, that is how you eat this."

"I heard this is your recipe?"

"Yea," Valli spoke with her mouth so full of stuff.

"That's why it's a disaster."

"*Ayyee*, don't act, yea? I know you like it. Sadly, you're the only one. A lot of people do not. They think it's too sweet," she said, taking another handful from the leaf.

"Easy there, I thought you brought the food for me,"

"Aw," she frowned and put it back on the leaf.

"You're suddenly taking me seriously? I thought we were joking around."

"So can I take some?"

"Nah."

"Well, too bad," Valli said and took some, nevertheless.

All through the meal, Karthik was contemplating if he should show Valli his painting. He didn't really know how she would react. He then decided to hell with it, he would show her. They finished eating and cleaned themselves in the spring. The Yaazhi was now half asleep.

"Lucky fella, gets to do nothing but eat, sleep and repeat the whole thing again," Karthik rubbed its big stomach. "Hey, can I show you something?" She took her to the cave.

"Did you find that moose sadhu?"

He was ready to show her his painting, but not ready to share about the sadhu. He laughed it off. They walked into the clearing with his painting. Valli walked near the rock and touched it softly, so as not to disturb the dye.

"This is a great painting of Mullai."

"Who now?"

"Mullai. The girl who danced along with me. Seems you like her a lot," Valli resolved, a wicked smile on her face.

"You know what, I should just…" he bent to pick up the dye left from the day before and threw it on her face.

"Hey, I just.." she wiped it off. "I can't see, you fool. Take me to the spring." After washing herself, Valli held Karthik's hand and moved a little closer to him. "Thank you for the painting, Karthikeya. It is beautiful."

"Yea, Mullai was a great model."

Valli picked some wet mud from the ground and rubbed it on his face.

"Nice, now I have to clean up. God, we are such children," Karthik complained.

"It's nice to be a child, now and then."

"You people never gave me the honey I asked for," Karthik complained.

"Why the hurry? You're staying for a couple of more days, right?"

"I mean..." Karthik sighed.

"Oh," Valli's face fell. "Come," she said and started walking.

"Where?" Karthik ran to catch up with her. The Yaazhi opened one of its eyes to see if it should go along but decided it was best to leave the two alone. Also, it couldn't handle their bickering any longer, so decided to just sleep without disturbance, finally.

Valli and Karthik reached a waterfall. Valli was silent throughout the walk despite Karthik trying to initiate conversation a couple of times.

"Here, your honey," Valli pointed to a tall tree, on top of which there was a bunch of bee hives.

"Valli, why won't you talk to me?"

"Why? Will that make you stay?"

"It's not that simple, Valli. If I were to stay, I'd have stayed in my home. I'm a nomad."

Lies, lies all of it. He remembered the sadhu's words.

"Alright."

Valli took out her slingshot, loaded it with a small pebble, and signalled Karthik to hide inside a bush. She followed him and hid in the bush as well before shooting the stone up to the hive that sat to the far right of the branch, away from the rest of them. She continued to hit it with a few more stones until a piece of the hive broke apart and dropped to the ground. They waited in the bush until all the agitated bees had settled.

"I'm sorry," Karthik decided to break the silence.

"Your loss that you won't get to see the sun festival."

"I'm not only missing the sun festival, Valli."

He wanted to stop talking. This conversation made no difference to his decision. Valli turned around and looked him in the eye. She knew what he meant.

"If you are willing to walk out on things, it shows that they never meant anything to you."

"I walked out on my family, Valli. It does not mean they meant nothing to me."

"I stand by what I said," she stood up. "Take your damn honey and scurry before you spoil Mullai's heart by giving her hope. You'd probably walk out on her too."

"Valli, I…" he realized he should stop talking. He was going to walk out on her. There was no point in this. He didn't have to justify his feelings to her. He walked up to the piece of the hive that fell down, and washed it a little under the waterfall. By the time he turned around, Valli had already left.

"Honey," he mumbled, and it felt as if he'd called her.

Chapter 07

Sun Scorched

It had been two days since he had left the Kurinji settlement. He felt guilty for not telling the people of the settlement before he left, but he let the thought slide. He was lying on top of the Yaazhi. It decided to join him; nevertheless, he was sure it would leave him at some point. They were walking through a large meadow when they noticed a huge crowd at a distance. There were at least five hundred people gathered around and the Yaazhi was moving towards them. The crowd fell silent seeing a Yaazhi approach. They all sat down and waited for the animal to pass by. All the music stopped and the fires were well-fanned to reduce the smoke.

As the Yaazhi came near, they realized there was a man on top of it. "Ayya, Karthikeya." A scream woke up the long asleep Karthik, and it didn't take long for him to figure out that he was in the middle of the sun festival. '*Well, what do you know*,' he thought as he climbed down the Yaazhi. He was expecting Valli to run up to him and was preparing the answers he'd give to an angry chief Nambi. What would he say anyway?

The little boy who'd called him ran up to him and jumped on him. He caught the boy and carried him on his hip. The boy was heaving, crying his heart out.

"It's alright, son. What happened? Where's Ayya Nambirajan? Where are your parents?"

He realized that only a handful of children and old people were running towards him. The people from the rest of the settlements had collected around and there was complete silence in the entire meadow, except for the cries of the people of Kurinji. In the crowd, Karthik recognized the old man he'd first introduced himself to – one of the elders from the Kurinji clan. He put the boy down and walked up to the elder. He touched his feet, and the elder man's face was too weak to fake a smile yet he did, wishing Karthik a long life.

"Ayya, where are the rest? Sorry, I could not make it to the festival with you all."

"It's okay, son. This is all of Kurinji now," the old man smiled. His smile shook Karthik's core being. If hopelessness had a smile, this was it.

"I don't understand."

"Neither do we, son."

The old man finally broke into tears and fell on his knees. The entire Kurinji clan cried, reminding Karthik of the cries that constantly echoed in their village's graveyard, night after night. No. No, no, no. He wanted to run off again. He wanted to scream and hide in the woods. He wanted none of this bullshit. Yet, he sat down near the old man, and he let him cry on his shoulders.

After a long time, the members of Kurinji sat down under a huge banyan tree with Karthik in the middle.

"The day after you left, which is two days before today," the elder blew his nose, whipped it out to the ground, and continued, "we were all doing our usual chores. The hunting party had just returned, well, you know that, don't you? Yea,

yea. You know. So, there was a lot of food and the village was getting itself ready for the sun festival. The chief had asked us, elders, to take care of the customs, and the entire village was bubbling with joy. The joy, however, lasted only until that evening. At dusk, right when darkness fell, came a bunch of ghosts. Probably a hundred of them, could be more. They came on horses and carried enchanted swords. They wore black robes and screamed like demons. Our guards and men fought valiantly but were no match for a hundred men carrying sorcery far superior to our sticks and stones. Hence, they fell in vain. We lost around 40 of our best soldiers and a lot of others were fatally wounded. They took our meat, our produce, men and women, and everyone who was in good physical condition. They left us and the wounded to die. They scorched the entire settlement to the ground and fled. The last we saw of them was when they rode into the woods with all our men and women locked in traps like big rooms, pulled by horses. We don't quite understand what happened, Karthikeya. All we know is that the Kurinji as we know and love, is nothing more than a graveyard now," he said in the most lifeless, bland and defeated tone. "Maybe getting trampled by the Yaazhi would've been a more honourable way to go," he concluded, looking into his palms.

"What about the chief? And his family?" How much more selfish could he get, Karthik wondered.

"Valli, our dear Valli, and her mother along with all our other women were taken. The chief was heavily wounded, so we had to leave him along with some thirty-odd injured men in what remained of our village. They're being taken care of by some of the older women now. We'll have to go back there. We wanted to skip the festival this year, but the chief believed that it took more than a bunch of men on horses to bring the morale of the clan down. So, he sent us to be a part of the ceremony," the old man scoffed. "What more does the man have to lose? His wife and daughter were taken, his left arm severed, his guts pulled out, and he still hasn't lost one ounce of that courage," he said, his voice suddenly becoming a lot bolder, pride oozing out. "Will you come with us? The chief really seemed to like you. He'll need some soothing words at this time. He hasn't cried once yet. I think he should, you know. He wouldn't cry in front of us. Will you come with us, Karthikeya?" The old man looked into Karthik's eyes with the last bit of hope he had in his existence. His eyes, probably dry from crying for the past two days, glistened in the sun. "Ayya, please come with us," he started crying again, his hands naturally folding themselves in a traditional prayer. "Please, please let the Yaazhi trample the rest of us to death this time."

Karthik agreed to go. He, along with the Yaazhi, the people of Kurinji, and a few dozen from the other clans started their journey towards the settlement.

A few old women were sitting outside one of the burnt-down houses, cleaning fruits. They looked up as a group of people marched towards them. They saw the Yaazhi, and stood up.

"Karthikeya?" one of them wondered. "Ayya Nambi, Karthikeya is here," she announced. From within the hut emerged a damaged Nambi. He smiled at Karthik, and beckoned to him. He also noticed the members of the other clans. He greeted all of them with his hands together. He then whispered something into the ears of one of the women.

"Ayya Nambi says that he cannot speak louder, but appreciates everybody coming here," said the woman. Then she listened to something else that Nambi said and carried the message to the people again. "He says that everybody can stay up in the caves, a short distance from here. We will provide you with fruits and honey for a snack. He's sorry that our contribution to the sun festival was a lot lesser than what we had planned."

"Ayya, our chief will take care of your clan until you and your men have healed enough. Please allow us," a young soldier appeared out of the crowd and stood near Karthik and the Yaazhi. Nambi called the two of them towards him and signalled the remaining crowd to rest in the caves. He then asked the women to serve them something to eat.

He brought the two men inside his abode, now almost burnt down to nothing, and sat them down near him. He struggled to sit and let out an audible groan. "Veera, my son, how are you? How's your father?"

"Ayya, we are fine. Sorry for not being of any help," the young man took the chief's hand. Nambi patted him on his shoulders and pointed to Karthik. "This is Karthikeya. A visitor from far away. He saved our settlement from the Yaazhi outside. He saved Valli and a bunch of other women." He grew sadder as he went on, "They took them, Karthikeya. I don't even know who they were or what they were. They had weapons we'd never seen before, and they had moving rooms or prisons or whatever they were, carried by horses. We lost a significant portion of the clan." He kept his emotions in check and cleared his throat. "This is what is left of it now. A bunch of old farts that don't have it in them to digest the fact that all their wards were stolen by the shadow of a ghost. No trace, no meaning. All of them just gone." He smiled a very defeated smile. "Oh, and this is Veerabaghu. My nephew. His father is the chief of the village that's on the valley. A very valiant soldier, and my favourite nephew," he smiled. Veera was a young boy, maybe seventeen or eighteen. Definitely three or four years younger than Karthik.

"Veera, can you please go check on your people and make sure they're comfortable? Also, assist the elders of the village in gathering fruits, if needed. Please?" Karthik requested and Nambi nodded in approval.

Veera left the hut.

"Ayya Nambi, sorry for your loss," Karthik began, breaking a long silence. Nambi was heavily injured and his wounds were dressed with herbs and some thin animal hide.

"Well, I am sorry myself. My sorry self is still alive, isn't it?"

"Be strong, chief. For your people."

"Whatever is left of my people, you mean, surely. I lost my daughter and wife, Karthikeya," the chief was getting emotional. "I saw them carry people of my clan, one after another, into these big cages and lock them up like animals. I saw my men slaughtered, I saw my children being kicked and thrown around like rag dolls. I couldn't rip each one of those bastards' heads off like I wanted to with my bare hands. I wanted to kill every one of those sons of bitches, but I couldn't. I have failed, Karthikeya. I have failed as a chief, and more so as a father and husband. I have failed my clan and my ancestors, Karthikeya," he cried on Karthik's shoulders, pointing to the now fallen Yaazhi skull. Beneath it was the half-burnt teak wood. He wanted to say something to the chief, but couldn't. What would soothe a man who had lost this much? In the hut, he saw Valli's garland, all dried up now. He cried a little too, it was all but a whimper.

"I will find her," he said, his fists clenched. The chief looked up, confused. "I will find Valli, Ayya Nambi. I will search the entire world, the ground under it, and the skies. If that's what it means, I shall do it, and I shall find her. I will find every man, woman, and child that was taken away from this land because this land fed me. This land and the people of this land have fed me and provided me with what little family I have, and I am in debt. If it means I spend all my life searching, if it means I die, if it means I never get to see the light of the day again, if it means anything, I will do it. I will do it for you, for the land, for the love that you'd offered me, and I'll do it for Valli. I will find her and bring her here, chief. I will," he said.

He had to. He had to look Valli in the eye and tell her that he wouldn't walk out on her, not again. He felt unworthy even touching a man like Nambi, who had just lost everything that meant the world to him, yet was feeding his guests some fruits while he spent almost all of his youth in meaningless philosophy.

"I will bring Valli back as well as the people of Kurinji, my chief," he said, holding Nambi's face. Nambi cried even more now, holding on to the wound of his severed hand. Karthik figured he was simply thanking him with hands together. Just as he touched Nambi's hand, he dropped on Karthik's shoulders. After a very long time, Karthik was near a human corpse. He wiped the tears off the chief's face and carried him out to the hut's entrance. The people around cried in agony at their fallen leader.

Nambi's funeral took place at the centre of the settlement. The eldest of the settlement asked the chief's closest male relative there to cremate his corpse after completing all the customs. It had been a long time since Karthik had been at a funeral, and this one was a lot different from the ones in his village. After everybody left for the cave, he picked up Valli's stone pouch from inside the hut and loaded it with some ash from the burnt corpse. He took some with his index finger and applied it on the centre of his forehead. His father used to apply ashes from cremated corpses all over his body and kept telling Karthik about how this is all that a human life ended up in, eventually. He always said that one shouldn't be afraid of death, but should be embracing it, for death truly comes only once. Karthik had now decided to go find Valli and the rest of Kurinji. He was, however, not sure what to do or where to start. He knelt down and prayed to the remains of the chief. "Wish me luck, Ayya Nambi."

He wanted to inform the people of the settlement properly this time. He climbed on top of the Yaazhi, and it moved to the cave. On the way, it stopped near the now completely burnt corpse, stood there for a moment, and then continued walking. When they reached the entrance of the cave, there was a brooding silence.

"People of Kurinji," Karthik began, now down on the ground. "I spent very little time with all of you. I wish to stay and would have spent more of it with you if I were like before – just a nomad. But now, I am a man who has a promise to keep. A man with a job to do. I got the privilege of sharing Ayya Nambi's last moments with him. I had the honour of witnessing a great man, one of the greatest soldiers I've met, and a valiant chief. Thank you for all your love. But now, you must leave. Leave for the village nearby and live with them. Veera, take these people safely to your settlement. Keep them safe, keep them with your people. Take care of my people, for they are the greatest of the greats that the land has to offer. And I, Karthikeya, shall return, after fulfilling the promise I made to the great chief on his death bed. I will rebuild Kurinji," he spoke and as he finished, the people of Kurinji dropped to their knees. Karthik dropped to his knees, falling at the feet of the people of Kurinji. Both Karthik and the people had got back what they had briefly lost a while ago. A purpose and their chief. Karthik, before leaving, walked into the sadhu's cave and took one good look at the painting before he left. He was going to fulfil the promise, but not like the painting said he would. He wasn't sure how he was going to do it. But more bloodshed was definitely not the answer. He was not a warmonger.

"Brother," he heard Veera call out to him as he climbed onto the Yaazhi again. "When shall we expect you? I would like to come with you, please?"

"No, Veera. I am not looking for a fight. I am simply on a mission to bring the people of Kurinji back. I have no use for more soldiers. Nor will any number of people with sticks and stones be able to beat a horde of killers with superior weapons." He felt the knife he'd taken from the Yaazhi's legs hidden in the small of his back. "You take them back to your village. I cannot tell you when I will return, but if I ever do, it will be along with the people of Kurinji. Remember Veera, these are the people left in the clan of Gods. The clan that killed a Yaazhi, the clan that paved the way for a beautiful life, in harmony with the environment, the clan that adopted me. Treat them with all the respect you'd give to the late chief Nambi himself."

Veera nodded. He was disappointed that the man was not the soldier he'd expected him to be. He wanted to go with him and tear down every mongrel that made his people suffer. But he was right. The people left alive couldn't possibly thrive on their own. They needed a place to be. A safe one. He'd drop these people off to his village, then go on his own voyage to save the people of Kurinji. None of this diplomacy, he swore. No. Diplomacy wouldn't bring justice to the dead.

Chapter 08

The Swamp and a Bunch of Swords

Karthik started his voyage with a heavy heart and a pouch of ashes. He carried with him everything he'd always had – his glider, spear, and bag. The Yaazhi went with him, though he was sure it would walk away anytime it pleased. One thing he had on him, a real novelty to even look at, was the knife he'd got from the Yaazhi's leg. Even the people of Kurinji had never seen metal before.

It was made of something he'd seen before; the people called it iron. Even he'd never seen it until a few years ago, and the first time he saw it was when he walked with a bunch of blacksmiths along the coast of the river Tungabhadra. He asked them what it was and they explained that the metal was dug from the depths of hell, forged in fire, and quenched in water. He noticed that the metal was far stronger than the stones that were usually used to make or sharpen weapons. If the lot that took the people of Kurinji had hundreds of swords made out of this metal, they sure were a very advanced race. And what was it that the chief and the people of Kurinji said about moving prisons? They were surely talking about some structure with a lot of wheels, pulled by horses. Wheels, metals, trained and not just tamed wild animals; whoever these people were, they sure were not an ordinary group of robbers or looters. They were something far worse. He stared at the knife and wondered if he really could keep his promise.

✣✣✣

Three months later, it all seemed like a blur to him. He had been following a trail, one that was on and off, left behind by the giant wheels. They had cut through entire forests and had left all of the places they crossed in a pitiful state. The Yaazhi was still optimistic, playful, and just as hungry. They often shared meals, and Karthik almost always slept on top of the Yaazhi. He had crossed a couple of other settlements, smaller than the Kurinji village, on his tracking expedition. The fate of those villages was the same as the Kurinji village, in fact, if he was right, it was a lot worse. Neither were there any people left in those places to narrate what happened nor was there any trace of the people who did this. He'd hoped that someday he would get a glimpse of Valli.

The duo of him and the Yaazhi were walking on a swamp, and he decided it was a good place to fish. He was hungry. He was still surprised that the Yaazhi was able to support its enormous physique with just leaves and fruits. He got off the Yaazhi.

"Alright big guy, I'll go get me some fish. Why don't you rest here and do what you do best? Eat some stupid leaves," he said.

The Yaazhi pushed him with its trunk and did just what he said it would do. It began eating some leaves. "You know, one of these days I'm gonna get tired being pushed around and I might just punch you in the face," Karthik said as he set his belongings down and went snorkelling. His spear helped him a great deal now that he'd modified it a little. He'd replaced the stone edge with the knife and tied it together with a piece of the animal hide. He'd used bee wax to stick it in its place, but kept the stone edge in his bag, just in case. He caught a few small fish but wanted one big fish so that he wouldn't have to stop often for food. He planned on stopping only once a day for his meal. The Yaazhi didn't really have to stop and eat, it just snacked all the way. He didn't expect to run into the horde anytime soon since he anticipated them to be a lot faster with horses and wheels. Unless they decided to camp somewhere. Even then, he doubted if they'd settle on a temporary camp for too long with a lot of captives. He wondered if he was walking into a dark, dark place with no return. He could not care less at this point. Everybody dies anyway. He took a little ash from the pouch now and then and put it on his forehead. The memories of his father, mother, his home, Valli, Nambi, Veera, and the dwarf sadhu tormented him a lot whenever he slept. He was barely holding on to his sanity.

He saw a big catfish moving towards the surface of the swamp and got ready to throw the spear at it. Just then, he heard the Yaazhi scream. The same way it had screamed when he first met him. He ran towards it.

"Stop it, he's mine," he shouted when he saw a bunch of men rounding it up with stones and clubs. He ran straight to the Yaazhi and stood on top of it, his spear and shield out. "He's not a wild one, mind you. He's mine."

"Don't bluff, nobody owns a Yaazhi," one of them called out from behind him. They were six men with the most basic weapons.

"I don't own him, you idiot. Of course, you can't own another being, and definitely not a Yaazhi. I happen to be the one he stays and travels with, so I protect him with my life. Your club goes through me before it touches my boy," he resolved.

"Easy there, men. Stand down," said a voice. Karthik turned around but found no one. Then the ground opened up. The ground, what? He looked closely. A man walked out of it. He was dressed in tiger hide with exotic feathers for a hat and held a stone spear. He had a sword made out of metal. "We're sorry, boy," the man said as he came out of the hole. He closed the door on the ground and it seemed like there was nothing there at all. The top of the door was laced with leaves and grass so it would blend right in with the floor. "We never intended to hurt the animal. Not that we can with just six men and a few clubs. The intention was merely to make it change its course and drive it to the other side of the swamp. He can't really walk on the ground here, you see?" he pointed out to the ground. There were a lot of thorny shrubs, probably grown there on purpose so as to stop people or animals from walking on top of these lands. "We don't think the doors are equipped to support the weight of a Yaazhi. We built them with something lighter on our mind, you know?" the man from the burrow said.

"Alright, got it. He won't move any further, and when I'm done hunting fish, I'll go to the other side of the swamp," he fanned his hands towards the ground and door. "Your houses?"

"Yes, young man. This is where we live."

"Good, finally someone alive on the tracks I've been following. Do you know anything about the horde that went this way some time back? They ride horses and carry weapons made of metal, just like yours."

"And they wear black robes. Yes, we know them. We know them a little too well. I also don't like that your spear bears its knife. How did you get it?"

"What? This is their knife?"

"Come down, I'm not comfortable standing outside for this long. My neck hurts from looking up for so long. Let's talk some more but in my shameful burrow."

He opened up the gate again, and all the men entered while he stood waiting for Karthik. By then, Karthik had got down and was talking to the Yaazhi, asking it not to go anywhere but stay in the same place. He pulled a fallen tree branch near him, one with a lot of leaves and ferns, and asked him to munch on it while he was away.

Then, he climbed down the burrow with his spear and shield. He was not walking into a random dude's weird-looking hut without protection. For all he knew, they could be rabbit people nibbling on human toes.

"So, tell me how you got the knife?" The man with the feather hat, who introduced himself as Kadalon, asked while taking Karthik into a seemingly long tunnel. There was no natural light and they had to use a lot of torches all the way.

"What is this place?"

"The one that has kept us alive, that's all I'll say," he replied.

The tunnel opened up to a large underground hallway with rooms on the sides. There were around nine rooms, and the centre of the hallway had a little fire pit that lit up the entire hall. In one corner, there was a pile of something with animal hide covering it, but from the shimmering piece of metal poking out of the hide, Karthik guessed they must be metal weapons.

"I must say, this is an impressive feat of engineering." Karthik genuinely could not comprehend the amount of work and precision it must have taken for these people to build this. "How is this not caving in?" he asked, looking up. "Oh," he exclaimed when he noticed wooden sticks, probably bamboo, laid down horizontally and vertically, on top of which the ground stood firm.

"Living like a meerkat is not impressive, young man. It's a curse. We're degenerating for deciding to do this," one of the men from the outside responded.

"Then why put in all the effort?"

"Enough. If you want us to talk, I suggest you talk first. Where did you get the knife from? Who are you, young man, and why are you in search of those cursed, cruel men?"

Karthik told them the story, all of it. He didn't like reliving it again and again, but it was not like he'd forget it if he didn't speak about it.

"I respect the fact that you want to honour your promise to a dead man, but I suggest you drop this little expedition of yours and go back to doing whatever you were doing before. This will only end in one way."

They were all sitting around the fire. One after another, a few people came out of the rooms on the sides. There were around twenty people around the campfire now.

"Well, it's not like being alive is going great anyway," Karthik casually tossed a dead bug on the floor up to the fire.

"Is that what you think happens when you get there? To that place? To that hell? Death? No, no, no. You don't understand, they don't kill you there. Death has to be easy, son, because we've all lived there, and nothing, nothing gets harder than life behind those wretched mountains."

"So you know where they live?"

"Is this guy deaf? I am gonna assume that this guy is fucking deaf because he ain't hearing anything I say. Don't go there, kid. They aren't sane people. Actually, they aren't people to start with."

"Is that why you hide here? You escaped from them and they'll come looking for you?"

"Listen here, you little brat. We didn't escape, we aren't hiding, and no, they aren't gonna be looking for a handful of slaves. We were skilled enough for them to let us join their little recruitment unit, to sharpen their weapons and maintain them while they continued killing with them. But let's say we took care of our buddies once we were sure that we were at a reasonable distance from the kingdom. We took out around thirty men, one after another, and when our cover was finally blown, our platoon of thirteen men fought their lot of seventy-nine men, head-on, and killed every one of those bastards. We lost four of our men, but hey, at least the rest of us nine are alive and thriving, eh? These people are the ones that were kept captive at the time with us, so we decided to take care of these poor fucks by providing them with a decent living here. And we live in a burrow because, well, we don't want to run into another horde of those flesh-hungry men. So, if you say anything that's marginally offensive to my valour or my men's honour, I will drink your blood."

"Do you say that as a threat or do you just like the taste of blood?" Karthik responded.

The nine men laughed. The rest of the people around the campfire were asked to go back into their rooms.

Chapter 09

Dungeons and Death Traps

"Look kid, you have heart. So, I'll tell you what happened. But if you tell our story to anyone and if it means that our place is exposed because I decided to tell a stupid young guy with a big mouth about one of the most dangerous places on the banks of the mighty ocean, I will personally come and skin you alive. I tell you everything I know and you leave us the hell alone, alright?"

"Deal," Karthik started listening, readying himself for some information about Valli, after months of absolute cluelessness.

"They call themselves the children of Suriyan, the Sun God. The asuras, if you will. Their race consists of ten thousand people or so we have heard. We don't know for sure. They live beyond Mount Kraunch. Now, do not go looking for a Mount Kraunch because they don't like people looking for them. There are no settlements anywhere near the mountain; there is nobody alive other than us that knows about the sooras, and nobody who knows about them leaves their kingdom. The mountain is governed by the king's brother. The mountain and the land beyond it, extending to the sea, is just like a shed if you will. An attic where you store meat. They keep all their slaves there, temporarily, before the slaves are categorized and put into different employments that support the actual city. The city of Mahendrapuri. The city of the sooras.

These assholes, the sooras, found out about the fire, the wheel, the metal, the medicines, and everything before the world did. And what did they do? They built a city two miles into the sea, where no big army could march to, and used Mount Kraunch to hide their city in plain sight, seen anywhere from the land. The mountain, oh you should take a look at these brainy bastards' engineering. They have turned a whole mountain into a watch tower.

As their population grew, they needed a lot of labour, you see. But these pretentious people would not dirty themselves with measly jobs like building, cleaning, cooking, and other silly things. No, no, they wouldn't. They need bigger houses, they need more metal, they need more and more food, and more slaves to do all this for them while they sit on their thrones and make art and drink wine. But more importantly, they know hardly anything but art and war, those brutes. So, they come out in hordes, on their horses, and in their robes, with metal weapons, and take in the people who can barely defend themselves against them. They call it a victory even."

The man grew visibly angry. "They have over five thousand slaves, from different parts of the peninsula, all working to build bigger thrones for them to sit their asses on. The place makes you forget who you are, kid, and makes you do the one thing they want you to do. Refuse, and you're thrown into a dark abyss with no food for who knows how long. They do this until you agree to do anything they say, anything at all, in exchange for just some pathetic food. Try to escape, dungeon. Try to form an alliance or friendship with the fellow slaves, dungeon. Ask for a little extra food, dungeon. You try to kill yourself, dungeon. Dungeon, dungeon, dungeon. Do you know how long I spent in the dungeon before executing this plan of ours? Do you know that on most of the days I forgot that the sun or time, or anything at all existed because I spent too long in the dungeon? Do you know how I had to swallow my pride and ask the same people that raided my village for some food?"

He gripped Karthik's shoulders and shook him as if he was waking him up. "That place is hell. Those people are ghosts and demons. And Mahendrapuri is a graveyard of the dreams of the slaves, with thrones only for the locals, made out of their slaves' bones."

"And they took my Valli there," Karthik was frozen, staring into the eyes of the man who was still holding him by his shoulders.

"And our entire village is still there. We cannot go there or save them. They're as good as dead. In fact, they'd wish they were dead. We wished for it when we were there," a man from across the fire replied.

"I'm not going to fight them anyway. I don't think killing is right."

"Well, with that attitude, you'd probably not even make it to the foothills of Mount Kraunch," one of them laughed.

"Also, please do not take your Yaazhi there with you. They'd enslave it too," another suggested, smoking his tobacco pipe. "We've heard that they have a hundred Yaazhis in their army. I heard my mom works in one of the Yaazhi camps, picking up poop and feeding them leaves."

"But hey, who are we to tell you what to do? Do go there and enslave yourself if you will or don't. Why do we care?"

"Well, great pep talk, you guys. I am hella motivated right now," Karthik stood up and dusted himself, ready to leave. "I think I'll pretend to be one of their lost soldiers, you know. I have a Yaazhi and a knife of theirs. I don't think they're gonna know all of their soldiers by face, given the fact that there are almost fifteen thousand people in the kingdom. So, I think I can get in, drop my boy in one of the camps, disguise myself as someone else, and roam around the city to find Valli, and get back out with her. What say?"

"I say horse shit, but whatever," the man in the back replied.

Kadalon put his hand up, stopping everybody else.

"Look, this is insane. You're volunteering to go enslave yourself, which we have no problem with. But at least get your plan as fool-proof as possible. We have a few robes from the soldiers that we killed and a lot of weaponry. Take everything you need, and tell them that your platoon died of a plague. They'll not inspect you any further, thinking you would have the plague as well. You will be kept in confinement and given medicine, just like everybody who enters the mountain. Once you enter the mountain, they will ask you a lot more questions about yourself, and the platoon that came with you. You're obviously going to screw that interrogation up, so they'll kill you there. They hate spies. If you can somehow bypass that interrogation and answer a few questions correctly, they'll let you in. So, I'll give you the details of the platoon that these fuckers were a part of."

He pointed to the pile of clothes and weapons. "Tell them you fell behind the platoon because the horse's leg broke, and you had to enslave a Yaazhi. Before you did all this, the platoon had already contracted the flu in one of the settlements and you found them dead on your way forward. Tell them you returned as soon as you saw that, and tell them you went nowhere near the bodies or the settlement. Once inside Mahendrapuri, you're on your own because we don't know how the place really works, except for the iron mines. We worked there. To start with, take a few of these weapons and tell the people in Mahendrapuri that you want them sharpened. Once in the blacksmith shed, ask for a slave named Devayanai. She's my sister, one of the best blacksmiths available in the shed. If you're so unfortunate that she's in the dungeon when you get there, you'll have to wait. They'd understand if you want to wait, they usually wait for the best slaves as well to get their job done. And for all this, you'll need something called kaachu. They don't help each other just like that, you know. They use a medium of exchange."

He showed him an iron disk, maybe as big as a lemon. One side had a mountain, and the other side, a building. "This is a kaachu, a coin from Mahendrapuri. This is how you buy food or get your work done there. I have lots of them, again, from the dead platoon. Finally, do not, do not take your black robe off in public. The black veil stays because even the people inside the city leave their soldiers alone. Stay in a chathram, the community hall, and if you pay them enough, you'll be given a separate room. Don't talk to anyone, do not stay in one place for longer than a week, and at any cost, do not wander around like a fool. Every step in Mahendrapuri could be your last if your cover is blown."

Kadalon kept talking as he provided Karthik with the weapons, coins, and robe. He gave away all the details as well as the names of the men from the dead platoon and asked Karthik to take the name of one of the dead soldiers.

"Also, you never met us. If you get caught, tell them you robbed one of their men and got all this."

"Why are you helping me with all this again?"

"Go on now, before I change my mind."

"Brother?" One of the men stood and walked to Kadalon.

"I know what you're going to ask. But these people. And there's…" he stopped talking and turned towards Karthik. "Go wait outside and make sure nobody sees you climbing up the door. I'll be right out," he said and waited until the boy went out. He then continued, "Look Izhavazhaga, I understand that we can join the boy. But once inside, we have no way out again. You know that even after all this planning the boy is still going to die in there, right? That's hell, Izha. I'm not betting our freedom on a silly boy."

"Freedom, brother?" Izha scoffed, stretching his arms out. "We were waiting for this for so long, brother. We were waiting for a chance to go in again, to be able to save the people of Neidhal. That was the plan when we got out. Go to the other villages, gather enough people and go back in to save our folks."

"And, and why didn't we do that, I wonder?" Kadalon asked. "Oh, I remember, because there were no other villages. There were no people left in our entire clan outside the confines of the mountain. We need an army to face those asuras, Izha, not one guy who's driven by his love for one woman."

"So, you want us to die in this hole, Kadalon?"

"At least you can die whenever you want here, do you understand?" Kadalon shouted.

"I'm going with the boy. The same story, the same plan you gave for the boy can work for two soldiers, yes?" Izha picked up a robe and a sword and stormed out into the hallway towards the entrance.

When Izha walked out, the rest of the crew followed him out and saw the boy sleeping on the Yaazhi. "Really, you fell asleep?"

"What? Me, no!" Karthik tried to stand up immediately, startling the sleeping Yaazhi. They moved at the same time, clumsily, and Karthik fell down, landing on his back. "Ow."

"Well, get ready to die for nothing, men," Kadalon called out to Izha for the stupidity of the plan that they'd made earlier.

"What? Who's dying?" Karthik asked as he stood up, dusting himself.

"Change of plans, kid. We're riding there with you. We know the place better, and we have our entire village stuck inside too. We don't hope to make out of there alive, but we'd have at least tried."

Karthik could not believe what he was hearing.

"Wait, y'all said it was a suicide mission when I wanted to go back in. Also, how about the plot holes in the plan with ten of us going in now? Did all ten of our horses break their legs together?"

"You've clearly not heard of death traps," Kadalon replied. "See, we're ten of the front-row soldiers. We rode into a bamboo stick laced with stones and weapons hidden beneath the surface and fell off our horses. Our horses broke their legs or injured themselves. And everything else is the same as planned. I still believe this is a suicide mission. Now the risk of being made out is ten-fold. So long as we tell the same story, as a crew, we would live long enough to go to Mahendrapuri. If not, we die on the mountain."

"You're always optimistic. That's what I love about you!" Karthik joined his hands together and bowed down a little. Kadalon pulled out a stone from his pouch and threw it on Karthik's head.

✣✣✣

It'd been a few months since Karthik's unit had started travelling towards the southeast. Karthik had grown really close to the nine soldiers and learnt that their primary occupation in their original village was fishing. They claimed to have built rafts called Kattumaram, strong enough to carry ten to fifteen people at once into the raging sea. He loved hearing about the sea or as the men called it, the Aazhi Perungadal. He figured this could be one of the reasons why the men chose the swamp lands to make their burrows in. There were a lot of fish there. Every time the unit crossed a water body, the men grew visibly excited and had fun swimming for hours. Wherever the unit ran into a mountain, Karthik simply could not resist climbing up to the summit and sitting there for a few hours.

The two parties, Karthik and the soldiers, understood where each came from, and what strengths each of them brought to the table. Kadalon and his crew noticed that Karthik really despised fighting, even if it was when they were just practising. He never fully let go of himself – which was one of the primary rules of fighting. Kadalon believed that Karthik was a far more elite warrior than he let others see because his footwork and grip were a lot better than some of his own crew, who were seasoned warriors.

Karthik noticed that unlike the people of Kurinji, these people knew how to use a spear. Not completely, but their snorkelling experience had taught them at least how to hold one. The unit moved at considerable speed, with Karthik on his Yaazhi, and the rest of the unit on horses. The crew also taught him how to ride on horseback. Karthik had mounted horses back at his home, but he'd completely forgotten how to ride one with ease. It took a lot of practice before he got back the form. Slowly, he learnt well enough to fight on horseback. Every time they practised, Karthik made it clear that if there was going to be a fight, he'd really not be of any use since his lack of attitude made him simply a show specimen, and of no practical use.

When asked why he didn't like wars, he mainly said that human life was a little more important than the reasons or causes of war. He told them about his home. They all tried to use his glider, but except for Izha, none of them could stick a landing. In fact, a couple of them fell from really tall elevations and sprained a few muscles. Karthik did have fun laughing at everyone who fell down.

Kadalon was a really good singer, and he and Karthik usually sang in the evenings after a tiring day. Their songs were in total contrast, and they noticed that their prayers were a lot different too. Karthik often thanked the Earth, while these men thanked the sea. Karthik really wanted to see what all the fuss was about, and a little part of him, though he was on a mission to bring back an entire clan out of what seemed like a literal hell, was excited to see the sea. He'd heard a lot about the roaring waves and the sands on the shore. Kadalon told him that he wanted to see snow once in his life. Karthik wasn't sure when he was going back but promised he'd take Kadalon with him when he returned.

"There," Kadalon pointed to a blue expanse and a mountain far away. "There's the sea and a part of Mount Kraunch that the people of Mahendrapuri use as a gateway to their city. And remember, you are not Karthikeya anymore, you're a part of the Kottravai's third legion, and your name is Moorgan."

"What does Moorgan mean, anyway?"

"An angry man."

"So I act all grumpy?"

"First of all, act your age. Then let's see about the grumpy part. Child."

"There's nothing wrong with being a child now and then," Karthik smiled, re-living a very distant memory. This is where she lived. He was going to meet her again. A lump grew in his throat, but he didn't want to get all mushy in front of the boys, so played it off and pushed the Yaazhi forward.

"Alright, we will camp here tonight. Stock up on as many leaves and water for our rides as possible, and hunt a large game that would last us at least four days. There aren't many plants after this point, and I don't want any of our rides to go hungry. Especially you, Karthikeya. You have a big mouth to feed," Izhavazhaga called out.

"Ah, ah, ah. Moorgan, and not Karthikeya. Not answering to Karthikeya anymore."

"He does have a big mouth," Kadalon sighed.

"Alright, alright. Unappreciative of my jokes, I see. Come on, buddy. Let's get you some travel snacks. Come on, brother," he patted the Yaazhi. They'd both developed a very peculiar bond over their travels. He learnt a way to communicate to the Yaazhi on how and at what speed to move in with his foot on the back of the Yaazhi's neck.

He learnt that the animal really did understand a lot of things, and was able to comprehend the danger and move out of harm's way. Although big, the Yaazhi was a mushy being, and often got vulnerable and possessive. They went out to gather a lot of leaves and straws from the shrubs and ferns around for them and the horses. They had to cover a lot of ground since they had instructions to collect food for almost four days. After collecting the food, they returned to their base to find that the crew had hunted a few monitor lizards and were cooking them.

"Here's all the grass for the animals," Karthik showed it off. It was piled on top of the Yaazhi, tied together with palm leaves.

"Nice. Come eat. After today, we set out on the final phase of our journey. Through the land of Palai. The deserts are gruesome. So gear up for some serious punishment from Mother Nature herself," Kaathavaraaya warned.

They had a filling meal and a peaceful sleep. The next day, they started walking on the desert sands. Karthik prepared a strip that went around the head and covered the eyes of the animals to protect them from the sand. The men wore their black robes since they'd got this close to the kingdom's entrance. Karthik was asked not to talk too much, and if he had any questions, he was asked to forget about the question altogether.

After three and a half days of tiresome waddling, they reached the foothills of Mount Kraunch.

Chapter 10

The Sea, the Guards, and the Howling Wind

On the very edge of the mountain, under a thorn bush, in very little shade, he saw a stout man sitting. He ran up to the man and knelt near him. The crew quickly followed him, not quite sure who the man was.

"Ah, Karthikeya. Nice, nice. You find yourself in good company, I see. The Yaazhi is here as well. What's up, big boy? Is this man feeding you well enough? Very troublesome and forgetful boy this one, you know. So, what's up with you all? The men of Neidhal, eh? Greetings, the lord of seas, Kadalon! How's life? I see that you've finally decided to crawl out of that burrow of yours. I see, I see…" the man just kept talking, occasionally scratching his head and beard.

"Alright, you know what, that's very creepy. This makes it seem like you've been following us," Karthik said.

"Yea, yea, I followed you on foot and managed to stay out of your sight for all this time. And surprisingly, I've managed to beat you here too. Oh, how innocent you are! No idea how things work, you know. No idea at all. Maybe for the good, maybe for the good. All is for the good, after all."

"Okay then, how do you know all this?"

"How is a question for later, Moorgan! What is the question of the hour? What are you going to do in there? Are you still resolved not to kill anyone? Because the ones inside the confines of these mountains are bound by no such rules. If you run into them with chains tying you to your stupid philosophies, you'll not only fail Nambi and your promise to the people of Kurinji, but also the hopes of two whole clans – the Kurinjis and the Neidhals. To be fair, there is a lot more at stake than just two clans here, you know. A lot, a whole lot is at stake. However, for the best of your understanding, let's just say these two are affected the most by whatever happens to you and your quest, because of how entangled they've become with your life. Fascinating, you see, how one day..."

"Okay! Okay! What, what should I actually do?"

"Learn the difference between staying true to yourself and staying true to an unwritten law that was probably coined by some other mortal in an era that did not have the same factors as today."

"And?"

"And bathe, at least once in two days. The hair gets really messy in this climate if you don't." He scratched his head some more. "And do not shy away from becoming the embodiment of truth itself. Though it seems like it is often, there are no two truths, there are only two perceptions of the same truth. How you perceive it is, of course, in your hands. But do not shy away from perceiving it in all its glory. Remember, a half-perceived truth is simply a lie in disguise."

"I mean, the guy is pretty slow and thick in the head. So, if you can stop talking metaphors and get to the point already," Kadalon was getting impatient. Who is the dwarf anyway, Kadalon wondered.

"Hi, I'm Agathian. A member of the muni folk."

"What? In the black magic?"

"Racist, but okay." He turned towards Karthik and continued, "To get straight to the point, perceive the truth that human life is invaluable in all its glory, and you would then be able to see beyond petty concepts like killing and living. Kill some bad people, Moorgan. Unleash your actual personality."

"Finally. Is this done? Have you imparted wisdom? Can we now go? The guards up there can spot us anytime," Izhavazhaga pointed to the mountain.

"Come on, relax. I'm just a beggar. Who's gonna be suspicious of me?"

The muni started walking off, scratching his head. He'd left a bag behind, and Karthik opened it up. In it, they found a bunch of Mahendrapuri coins.

"Some beggar," Kadalon wondered as he split the money into ten equal parts and gave it to the crew. They were finally ready to go into the mountain. Karthik was again instructed not to ask a lot of questions, no matter what he saw inside. He agreed.

After months of travelling, Karthik was finally relieved that at least he was in the same place as Valli. She was taken through this place as well. He had no idea where she was taken from here. She could be anywhere in Mahendrapuri, but he was standing where she once stood, not very long ago. Had it been a year? Maybe more than that. He couldn't care less. If it was going to take ten more years to find her, he would. He would find her and the rest of the Kurinji clan and get out of the place. How? *Kill some bad people, Moorgan.* He heard the voice of the muni. *Unleash that actual personality of yours.* Oh, he hoped not to. If he could weasel out of the whole place without having to use his spear even once, he'd be grateful. As agreed upon earlier, Kadalon would do all the talking, and Karthik 'would not talk at all', and answer only when questioned specifically. This worked for him because there was a lot for him to take in. Kadalon was right.

These magnificent people had carved an entire mountain into their watch tower. They entered through a huge gate, tall enough for at least four Yaazhis to stand, one on top of another, and enter without any problems. The entrance was guarded by two big gates, which were now open. There was a long queue of people and vehicles waiting at the gates. Karthik saw the moving cages that chief Nambi had told him about. These cages were full of livestock and people. The people looked tired and hopeless. Slaves, all of them would come to be. He tried not to dwell on it too long. The gates led to a tunnel of the same height, extending possibly to the other side of the mountain itself. He saw a lot of staircases on either side of the tunnel, climbing to the very top of the mountain. There were a lot of entrances, spread throughout the staircases. He assumed that these entrances were rooms where the guards stood, keeping watch on the people that came by. He counted the number of floors – there were thirteen floors of rooms. A very complex structure of catacombs must connect these rooms from the inside, he assumed. Were there stairs connecting these floors from the inside as well? He couldn't know, but there must be. He was amazed by how precise these structures were, and the fact that they were inside a mountain made it all surreal. Sons of bitches carved the mountain inside out. Truly a magnificent clan, and an impeccable feat of engineering. There were countless torches and lamps on the walls of the tunnel, and hanging from the ceiling. He noticed a deep hum throughout the tunnel. Unlike the hums in the caves that were constant and mild, these hums rose and fell with a steady tempo. He noticed at least a hundred guards in the tunnel, all equipped with metal gear. Armours, weapons, and even shields. Even Karthik and Kadalon's unit had all these but they did not have the crowns these guards did. They were stopped a couple of times by the guards, once at the very entrance and once in between. Kadalon showed them everything they had and answered all the questions they asked. The guard in the middle called one of the others standing on the staircase and asked him to take Karthik and his party somewhere to keep them in isolation until the medical team arrived. The guard on top signalled that they come up. The ten men slowly climbed up the steep stairs. They were taken inside through one of the entrances, and it was hard for Karthik to believe that he was inside a mountain. The entrance opened up to a huge hallway, shaped like a pentagon. On either of the sides, there was an entrance leading up to another room, and a ladder at the centre of the pentagon with a hole on top of it. As they walked to one of the doors in the hall, Karthik looked up the hole to see that it extended through a lot of floors, probably connecting the entire mountain. So, he was right. The floors and rooms were all connected, from the outside as well as the inside. How long did it take to build this thing? How many people did they put into this project? The slaves probably worked on it. The reality made him hate the structure a little, but it truly reminded him of the potential of the human race. The hum had now reduced, but he kept hearing the roar rise and fall at constant intervals. Oh. The sea. The waves. He couldn't wait. At least the guards couldn't see him smile a little behind the black robes. He would see the sea and then, her.

Chapter 11

Ferries and Folk Lore

After a thorough investigation and solitary confinement of three days, the crew was finally brought back down to the mountain tunnel. They'd been given a lot of medicine in those three days, and Karthik had never felt better. He spent the three days hearing the sounds of waves crashing into the shore again and again. The sea never gets tired, Kadalon often told him during their journey for the past several months, and now, he finally understood what it meant. The sea never gets tired, really.

The tunnel was still full of people and vehicles, but this time the guards took the unit through a path that was separated by barricades. The soldiers used this path to move in and around the tunnel, exclusively for faster movement. The speed lane, they called it. Karthik started answering to the name Moorgan, and had become a soldier of the Kottravai army's third legion. This was one of the few places he'd noticed that the main God was a female. There were quite a few female Gods, almost always accompanied by their male counterparts. But here, it was just Kottravai. As they made their way through the tunnel, the sound of the waves got stronger and stronger.

Finally, the tunnel seemed to come to an end because they were able to see some natural light. All of a sudden, it opened up to a beach.

"Welcome to the sea, mountain boy," Kadalon whispered into Karthik's ears.

Karthik could not speak. There was just water everywhere. And sand. For as far as he could see, he only saw the two. He turned around a little to identify that Mount Kraunch made an arc, both its ends touching the shore. There were iron gates at both ends, going into the sea. The tunnel truly seemed the only way into this place. He turned around and tried as hard as he could to simply not fall on his knees and cry. What is this place? How had he never seen a sea, ever? Why did he not live by the sea? Why did he never see the waves before? Oh, the beauty. The wind. The waves. The water. The blue expanse of absolutely nothing but water. He'd seen pretty big rivers before. He was born near the Ganges, for all he remembered, but this. This was the sea. The place where all the rivers ended up pouring their waters. He could not speak. He was transfixed by the sea. They were walking towards it, to the massive-looking wooden structures stationed on the banks of the sea. The boats, he remembered. "We're going to ferry number fourteen. Come fast." Izhavazhaga pushed Karthik ahead into the 14th ferry – he could not believe he was going into the big blue sea. He wanted to jump and dance and sit there to watch the sun set into the sea. He had to play it cool, though. At least his black robe hid his face. He stood on one edge of the ferry and felt it sway, moved up and down by the waves beneath. He stood there with his big Yaazhi, on a much, much bigger boat. There were twenty other boats standing parallel to his ferry, and the water simply moved all this weight up and down, playing with it like a child with a ball. He looked down at the sea in awe, watching how the boat moved in it, tearing through the sea and the waves. It was the Yaazhi's first time on the boat as well, so it was swaying a little, struggling to find its balance. He saw that an entire city was built way into the sea, and they were sailing towards it. Had there been land there before? Or did these guys just *build* land? He wouldn't be surprised if they did, after seeing what they'd done with Mount Kraunch.

After an hour of sailing, they reached the city's port. A lot of ferries and a lot of guards were stationed right at the entrance of the port. There were security checks again, and Kadalon took care of it all. They were taken to a rest-house, right next to the port and a man offered to tie their rides onto the shed. The ten men took two rooms, and after a while, all of them met near the sea.

"So, the sea?" Kadalon asked.

"This is amazing," Karthik said, grinning from behind the veil of the robe.

"Alright, I think we're free to roam around anywhere in the city, but I suggest we do not go to the places near the main palace. That's where the royalty lives. I think we don't want any more spotlight than what we've already received. We can roam around in these veils, pretty much unnoticed, anywhere other than the main palace or near it. I have informed the authorities that we are pretty tired from all the ruckus our platoon faced during the last voyage, and need a three-month break from any more duties. They were okay with it. I guess only the slaves are asked to work against their will. These guys are pretty kind to a fellow local. So, we will split up; that way we can meet more people. Find every person that you want to rescue and keep track of them. Remember, everybody that we want to get out of here is a slave. They shouldn't speak to you or they'll be in unnecessary trouble. It'll also blow our cover. So, please keep a safe distance. Every week, we meet at the blacksmith's workshop at the other end of the city, near the Kottravai temple. Do not stay in the same place for too long, and do not spend all your money on things you wouldn't need. Always remember that you are in a disguise, and do not do anything that'll attract attention. No hookers, no drinking in public bars, and no temple visits. Finally, no talking too much. We're here to rescue our people and get the hell out of this hellhole. We aren't sure how to do it yet but will find a way soon. I am working on a theory, but I am not sure of it yet. So, does anybody have any questions?" The unit stood still, so he continued. "Good. I'm moving out of the rest-house here to find a place in the city. It would be better if I stayed with Moorgan, at least for a week or so," he pointed to Karthik for emphasis, "because he's new here. Two soldiers roaming together shouldn't be a problem. No eyes on us. But the rest of you, please consider staying alone, stay in pairs if you please, but never stay as a group. Two is the sweet spot we can operate in, alright?"

Moorgan and Kadalon – now the soldier of the Mahendrapuri army – Karuppu, packed their bags and left the rest-house. "So, what is the deal with these people anyway?"

"Well, basically they're all animals. That's what their deal is. But to be more precise, Mount Kraunch, and the city of Mahendrapuri are ruled by a duo of brothers. Their grandfather was a very well-known sadhu, Ayya Kashyappar. To think that these degenerates are from the bloodline of such a man is a shame. The brother duo got the secret to technological advancements from the people that came from afar, a distant land. They used to sell stolen sea salt to the pirates and other civilizations around it. They made a lot of acquaintances across the seas, and both these cultures that revolved around robbery made a really good pair. They shared information and technology from around the world with the people of Mahendrapuri, who were then known as the Palai clan, while they got a place to get salt. Sea salt is still a rare delicacy and not a lot of people have access to it.

We, the Neidhal clan, found a way to produce salt from the seawater and taught it to the people of Palai when they asked for a way of occupation. They traded it with the devil and got rich sooner. It is folklore that the leaders of the clan, the now ruling king Soorapadhman, Chief Vajranaka's son, made a pact with the God of the water, from whose hair all of the world's water comes, and the Goddess of the lands, from whom all of life came to be, to not be killed by anybody but their son, a son born without any union. In return, he promised to live not on the land and not on the sea. So, he lives on land that they built on the sea. Weird, weird stories revolve around the success and the valour of the asura bloodline, but I simply believe they are geniuses with an industrious mind and a cold heart."

"That I agree. No wonder the work on Mount Kraunch was the child of a thousand genius minds and countless pairs of industrious hands."

"Only the ideation comes from there," Kadalon pointed to the palace, "everything else is done by the slaves."

"I figured."

"I also wanted to ask, who was that? The muni we met outside the mountain?"

"I don't know, man. He's been following me, I guess. He knows everything that I do."

"Munis are weird people, my friend. But they speak the words of Gods. Remember what he told you. Be ready to kill a bunch of bad people."

Karthik smiled it off. He was absolutely in love with the city of Mahendrapuri. The name meant 'A Beautiful City'. It truly did live up to its name, this one. All of the buildings in the outer ring roads were pale white, and he learnt from Kadalon that the floating population of the city lived on the edge. The merchants, the ferry riders, the soldiers that worked on the city compound patrol, etc. As you move closer to the centre of the city, the colour of the buildings became increasingly blue, and the residents of these buildings became increasingly important to the city. The royal palace, built at the very centre of the city, was huge. They hadn't gone to the inner layer of the city since it required getting a lot of permissions and they weren't having any of it. Karthik suspected that if seen from above, the city's colour choices would be very aesthetic – lighter on the edges, growing darker towards the centre, with just one really big building at the very centre. These people had a rigid adherence to geometry and symmetry in their construction and art. Each layer of the city, on the opposite side of the port, had a section of it dedicated to the slaves. Karthik and Kadalon decided to explore the city further and learnt about the culture and laws as even Kadalon had not seen this much of this magnificent city. The only two things that the 'owners' did not do to their slaves were rape or kill. Rape was considered a serious offence to Mother Kottravai, the land's deity. The offenders were executed after a trial, and their execution took place in the middle of the roads. Even the king wasn't allowed to touch a slave, or anyone for that matter, without consent. The slaves and the locals clearly lived in different worlds altogether, even though they lived in the same city. There were beautiful sculptures all around the city, fresh water fountains, wide and clean roads, tall buildings, and some fields for agriculture as well. There were carts pulled both by men and horses. The funny thing was that it cost less to travel on a cart pulled by men than on a cart pulled by a horse. The duo usually parked the Yaazhi wherever they stayed, and used a couple of rented horses to get around the city. Nobody bothered them, since the guys simply had a lot of money and no interaction with anybody who had power or authority.

Chapter 12

Freedom and Slavery

"So, is that everyone from our village?"

"No. If I'm not wrong, the population of our village was around 324. We only have around 290 people identified and located. The rest we have no idea about."

"Did you include the nine of us, you idiot?" Kadalon asked Thuduppan.

"Oh."

"Goddamn it, how am I going to pull off a heist like this with these ass hats?" he sighed. "Okay, enough of looking for people from just our village. Keep looking for members of our clan from nearby villages as well. Kandhagan had participated in a lot of boat races across villages, he must know a few. Keep him company and search some more. Where is he anyway?"

"He said he was staying near the Yaazhi station in the north wing. Not sure about which ring he stays in."

"Okay. You wait here and when he comes, join him."

"Kadalon?"

"Yes?"

"It's been three months since we came here. We're also running out of money. We can last another month or two. What is the plan?"

"Even we're running out of money. But we aren't ever going to come back here, ever again. And there's no guarantee that we'll be making out of this place alive as well. So, we stay here as long as we can and try to take as many of our people with us. No man is left behind, no matter how rough the sea is, remember? Search for little jobs, guarding, cart pulling, carrying pallakks. But do not stay in any job permanently. I'm also praying to the lord of the seas that the army does not call us back in for their work. If they do, we have no choice but to go and come back here along with the platoon. However, I don't think we'll ever be able to do that without getting our covers blown. So, we'll have to hurry up. We probably have to last here for a couple of months more, but what happens after or within these months is in the hands of Matha Kottravai herself."

"So, your sister, eh? One of the best blacksmiths I've ever seen! Not that I've seen many, you know? But how did a fisherwoman turn into a blacksmith? One that works on knives and swords?" Karthik asked as he walked out with his newly sharpened sword.

"We used to construct boats, remember? We started collecting metal scraps from the sea bed near the port and making anchors and sail rods from metal. These guys generate quite a few kilos of waste metal every now and then and dump it into the sea every month or so. She was the one who found out about the scrapyard in the sea, and she's the one who taught us how to work with metal."

"Nice. She's pretty strong."

"Karthik, you and I are splitting up," Kadalon started.

"We are?"

"Yea. I have some ground to cover on my own. How about you? Do you have someplace to be?"

"I have so far located 170-odd people, out of which I'm really sure about a hundred being former residents of the Kurinji village. The other 70 just look like people I know from different settlements. I haven't seen Valli or her mother yet. I've got only a few places left to search, apart from the inner circle and the palace."

"We are not going into the palace, no matter what."

"I didn't say I am planning to, just stating facts."

"Alright, you look in the places you said you've not looked into yet. Keep an eye on the docks, and see if there are any of your friends working there. The Yaazhi shed, the fishery, the house of sculptures... Keep looking. We have a month left, alright? I'm not sure, but I guess we're going to have to move in a month. Keep coming here, every Friday."

Karthik nodded. He was starting to get worried if he'd ever find Valli. This whole journey had been for her. He looked up to the palace. Was she in there?

That evening, Karthik was at the Kottravai temple. The temple was carved out of a rock, but they'd brought in the rock from someplace nearby. There were a lot of sculptures throughout the city, in fact, at least two on every road. Mostly, they were sculptures of animals, dancers, the king and his brother, and a few other Gods. But this temple's sculptures were phenomenal. Matha Kottravai's huge statue with four hands stood at least ten feet tall. She held a machete in one hand, a sickle in the other, a head in the third while the last hand held a chain made of little skulls. Even the chain was sculpted in rocks, with intricate details like the thread of the chain, the small skulls, and a lot more. She was sitting on a desert lion, with her tongue out. The details in the sculpture were amazing. The stone in front of Kottravai's statue stated that the structure was a gift from the king to his people. It was sculpted by Princess Asumugi. He'd learnt that Asumugi was the younger sister of king Soorapadhman.

"Princess Asumugi arrives at the great Kottravai temple. Arriving, the princess herself, the legendary beauty, and an extraordinary artist, Princess Asumugi."

The announcer at the temple blew his horn.

'*Well wow, speak of the devil, huh?*' Karthik thought.

He moved to the side of the temple and decided not to do anything but simply exist in silence and observe what was happening. He would've moved away and left by this time if Kadalon was with him. He felt freedom in the air.

The princess arrived on top of a Yaazhi in a chariot draped with silk. The rider of the Yaazhi had two hooks, one on each ear of the Yaazhi, and pulled the hooks to bring it to a stop. Karthik assumed the Yaazhi turned towards the direction the rider pulled the hook in and stopped when both hooks are pulled. These hooks, attached to long sticks that the rider held, were pierced into the Yaazhi's earlobes. Hence, pressing them forward would mean forward for the Yaazhi, he assumed. He'd never been on a Yaazhi ferry, so he was learning this just now. The driver rested the sticks on his shoulders and lifted his arms to hold the two levers on the chariot. He pulled them down, and two ladders dropped down from the bottom of the chariot to the ground, on either side of the Yaazhi. These people liked showing off their engineering in every way possible. How had they built the lever? How was it connected to the ladder? How would it retract? Karthik had so many questions but decided to observe further. Four women got down from the Yaazhi. Karthik assumed one of them was the princess as she was the only one who wasn't covered in white from top to bottom. The princess wore a red bottom and a green top, and her face revealed only her eyes. Nothing but eyes were visible in the four women and they all wore silk. Silk was a gift from Egypt, and only the royalty got to use it. Karthik was surprised that even the slaves in the palace got to wear silk. After the women got down, the rider started retracting a pully, and Karthik assumed that these ropes went through the ladder and retracted them. As he pulled the rope, one by one, the steps of both the ladders retracted in unison. After the last step was in place, the rider moved the initial levers in the other direction, and the ladders pulled themselves under the chariot. He and the Yaazhi moved out of the temple after the princess commanded him to, with just a hand gesture. A priest, wearing a black-hide bottom and some animal teeth on a chain around his neck, appeared from within the temple, and walked into the room with the Kottravai statue. There were bells ringing, drums playing, and horns blowing, signalling that the pooja for Matha Kottravai had started. After the brief incantation of mantras, the priest came out with a plate of red powder, held it in front of the women, and bowed down. Everybody else bowed down too. Karthik looked confused for a bit but immediately blended in and bowed his head. He peeked a little to see what was going on; there wasn't a single person who had their head held up. The princess then unwrapped her face mask and applied the red powder on her forehead, vertically. Oh, this was a tilak. His mother usually applied it on her forehead, in a round shape. He saw the woman, her beautiful face. She was dark, and her cheek bones stood out like they were carved on rock. She held gaze like a lion, and turned around to look at him. *Shit.* Just as he was about to lower his glance, he saw the three slaves take their masks off to apply tilak as well. Valli. *Shit.* He saw something shimmer in the distance from the opposite side. A guy moving stealthily across the crowd with a metal knife caught his eye. He did not have a robe on him and was dressed in a brown hide, usually something the slaves wore. *Shit.* Karthik noticed that he seemed familiar, and as he began running towards the princess and her party, Karthik began running there too. Valli was there, with the princess. He had to save her. Karthik threw his shield at him; by now the crowd had started running amok too. The shield hit the guy on the head and he fell down, but continued to pursue the woman. Karthik now noticed that the man was the leader of the Kurinji hunting party, but he didn't know his name. He pulled his sword out, pounced on the guy, and pressed the sword against his neck as he continued to resist. By now the princess's guard had run into the temple and surrounded the women. Everybody else was asked to leave the facility immediately. Karthik was trying to not get the Kurinji man killed. "Stand down," he whispered.

"And go back to scooping Yaazhi poop in the palace? Stand there and watch my clan's princess slave away as a stewardess? I will kill all you fuckers."

"Stand down," Karthik pressed his sword a little more on the man's neck, noticing the guards were running towards them. The guy still tried to wiggle his way out, grabbed Karthik's veil, and pulled it down. *'Shit,'* Karthik thought before he put the veil back and covered his face again, rolling onto his side. The guards ran in and took the guy away.

Karthik wanted to scurry out of this place. He covered his face with his hands and started walking out quickly.

"Soldier," he heard a woman calling out. Well, if it wasn't the thankful princess. He stood there, looking down. Kadalon would kill him if he knew what was happening.

"How did you know he was coming? How did you have enough time to respond? Which rank do you serve in?"

"Oh, so no thanks?" he just blurted out impulsively. Shit. He had to keep his mouth shut. The princess was taken aback, for nobody had the audacity to talk back to her, not this way at the very least. She stared at him for a second, saw him holding his veil to his face with his hand, and trying hard not to look like a man who had just said something he shouldn't have. She started laughing. Karthik tried to nervously join in and hehe'd a bit.

"I'm sorry. I forgot I was talking out loud."

The princess laughed even more.

"You were peeking, weren't you?"

"I mean…"

"Yea, yea, you were. A lot of people do. I saw you peek a little but couldn't see the other guy because he came from the back. Low life. But hey, thank you." She joined her hands and bowed down a little.

"It's an honour," Karthik did the same, and his veil fell down. Valli saw him and gasped a little. Had they taken him in as a prisoner too? She was happy for so long, thinking that at least he hadn't been captured. But are slaves taken in as soldiers? She was confused, but lowered her gaze and stood still. "I'm sorry," he muttered as he bent down to pick up the veil and hold it against his face.

"You're surprisingly clumsy for a soldier."

"I mean, not everybody is blessed with hands as steady as yours," he pointed to the statue. "It is beautiful."

"Are you only seeing this now, soldier?"

"Only now have I had the opportunity to thank the artist for something this wonderful."

Valli was fuming. What was happening here anyway? Does he know she's here? He wouldn't, right? How would he? But he peeked. So had he seen her? She also felt bad for Sangamithran, the man who tried to overpower an entire fleet of soldiers and kill the princess. What the hell was he thinking? And finally, why the hell was Karthik flirting with Asumugi? There was not one good thing about this day.

"Meet me in the palace courtyard tomorrow," the princess said as she turned around.

"I, I think, I do not have enough clearance to enter the inner circle, princess," Karthik replied. The princess was surprised that she was not addressed as the highness but liked that the guy was simply speaking his mind.

"What is your name, soldier?"

"I'm Moorgan."

"Alright, Moorgan." She pulled out a coin from her pouch and gave it to him. "This will give you access to anywhere in the city. So, come meet me in the palace courtyard tomorrow morning. You might want to stitch your veil, by the way. Doesn't look good on a royal guard."

"Thank you," Karthik said. "I will be there. Do you know a good tailor around, by the way, because I don't. I mean…"

"Silly fool," the princess laughed and climbed onto the stationed Yaazhi. Silly? He really did not know any good tailors around. Also, what would Kadalon think about all this? He really had no idea where anybody from the crew was staying. Oh, what had he got himself into?

Chapter 13

The Blue and the Pearl

That night, Karthik went back to his hotel, spent some time with the Yaazhi, and fed him some palm leaves. He rarely got time to spend with the Yaazhi nowadays. Wherever he went, he requested the people in charge of the stay not to tie the Yaazhi down and assured them that it wouldn't wander anywhere on its own. The Yaazhi was always happy to see its friend and was fortunately fed well.

He went to his room and sat down on the animal hide that was placed in one corner. He took out the coin that the princess had given him and even in the dark, saw that it was lustrous. The coin had the same palace and mountain embossed on it, which he now knew were the blue palace and Mount Kraunch. But it was not an iron coin like the ones that he had. It was a yellow metal, one he'd never seen before. He rehearsed all of his backstories and the answers he'd given at the entrance of Mount Kraunch, just to be consistent.

The next day, he woke up early, collected his black robe from the tailor – he had finally found one the previous evening – and walked to the inner circle. He was not particularly nervous but was not at ease either. He knew he was walking into an absolute blind spot. He had no information about anything inside the inner circle and was confused as to why he had been asked to come there. Royal guard? Was he getting a promotion for saving the princess? He walked up to the big gate, which divided the innermost circle and the rest of the city. All other divisions of the city had five entrances and five exits, but he assumed this was the only way into the inner circle. Just like the single entrance into and out of the slave camps. When asked why he was there, he explained that the princess had asked him to come to the courtyard and produced the yellow coin. The guards let him in, no questions asked.

Just when he thought he'd seen everything that the city had to offer, he was thrown into what he felt was absolute heaven, because no amount of human effort could've produced something this beautiful and magnificent.

The palace, the blue palace of which he'd only seen half from the far corner of the city, he got to see it up close now. He simply stood there, moved by the absolute engineering marvel it was. There were artificial waterfalls on both sides of the palace, which was built in the middle of the city, with a moat around it. The palace sat on a piece of land of its own, right in the middle of the sea while a drawbridge connected it to the rest of the city. The moat looked so pretty with a lawn around it. There were five small barracks surrounding the palace, adjacent to the inner side of the wall. Roads connected these barracks straight to the lawn, and there was a platform around the lawn. There were two big statues of Yaazhis on either side of the palace's entrance, designed to be water fountains. There were plants and sculptures everywhere.

As he walked into the palace, he was stopped every hundred feet or so and asked about his purpose of being there. The yellow coin opened every gate there was, and every soldier allowed him without any further questions. He was guided into an empty courtroom. The princess walked in after a while, accompanied by her three servants. '*Valli,*' he thought. Valli saw the soldier and figured it was Karthik. But what name did he introduce himself with? Moorgan? So, was he here undercover?

"This place is wonderful, Princess Asumugi."

"I know. I designed most of it."

"I should've known," Karthik bowed out of sheer respect for her artistic genius.

"Did anyone even dare to frisk you?"

"No. Your little souvenir saved me a lot of time and dignity."

This guy never ceased to amuse Asumugi. A soldier of such low ranks speaking of dignity? "Copper. A little gift from our allies. You can probably buy the entirety of the outer ring with that one coin, you know. You can keep it."

"Thank you." Well, there go his worries about his finances for the rest of his stay in Mahendrapuri. "Why am I here?"

"Because I wanted you to be," the princess laughed. "And, I spoke to my brother. Told him what happened. My life, Moorgan, is far more valuable than a copper coin. It's more valuable than the whole city, and every other settlement in the entire world. So, I have decided to repay you with a job inside the palace. My brother is okay with it, but unfortunately, Banukopan and Singamugan, two of my family members, doubt your prowess to be in the service of the royalty."

'*So, she has basically got me an interview that I did not ask for,*' Karthik thought.

"I've got you a chance to prove yourself worthy. You will fight our lions, just two of them, in the arena. Banukopan will watch you fight them, to death or not, I'm not sure, but he'll decide whether you get to work for the court or not."

"So, throwing me into a pit with a couple of lions. A very novel way to thank someone who saved your life, I see. Thank you, Princess."

"You talk too much, Moorgan. For some reason, I find you amusing, but I assume a soldier of the Kottravai legion never shuns away from a battle."

"I am a little orthodox. Shunning away from reward is part of my character. I refuse to accept this. The coin though, I'd be willing to take."

"Tell that to the lions, please, Moorga? I saw you pounce on the man. I know an able soldier by their stance. And wherever there is an ability, it has to be made use of to make Mahendrapuri, heaven on Earth. Don't worry, you'll be paid well. Just don't die to the lions."

Karthik was escorted deeper into the palace by two soldiers wearing red robes while the women walked in front. He checked if he was geared up for this. Sword, check. Knife, check. Shield, check. Armour, check. Cool. So, this is it. Just a couple of lions, and he'd be in the courtyard, hearing the daily proceedings of the legendary city, Mahendrapuri. Despite his fear that Kadalon would probably be hella mad at him for whatever has happened, he really thought that it couldn't get any better than this. He could carry information about every decision that the army and the government made to help Kadalon plan the heist better.

He entered an arena, a pentagonal one, which from his observation of the geometry of the city so far, was at the centre of the palace. There were a lot of seats around the area, and the area itself had a lot of rooms on the sides, and iron gates led under the seats. He revised his observation a little. Not only were the locals and slaves living in two different worlds inside the same city, but the locals and royalty lived in two different worlds as well. Karthik walked into the arena and got ready to fight. Though it'd been a long time since he had actually fought, it was never difficult for him to fight. *Unleash that actual personality of yours.* He heard the voice of the muni echo in his head and closed his eyes for a bit. *He was alone in the cold, and he was a baby. There were hungry snow leopards and eagles waiting there, waiting for him to die.* His body raged. He opened his eyes, took his sword and knife out, and crouched. He saw two desert lions on the other side of an iron gate. He saw their eyes and glimpsed in them what he had seen in the eyes of the snow leopard that day, on the banks of that river. Bloodthirst. He forgot that he was a man in a city and went back to that familiar feeling. He was a predator. The ultimate predator. If he put his mind to it, nothing could survive his wrath. He waited for the door to open, and it did. The two lions ran at him, one faster than the other. He snarled at them, leaping to the side, away from the line of attack. He quickly rolled beneath one of the lions, and with his knife, tore its stomach. The blood spilled all over him. Ah, how much he loved this smell. How much he'd missed it. The smell of blood. The lion fell down, but quickly got up, limping. The second lion sprang up to his neck, but he kicked it down. He swung his sword, brought it above his head, and waited for the two to regroup. He loved playing with his food. Always. The lions flanked him, the injured one was to his right. He switched the knife to his right hand and the sword to his left, and crouched again, snarling. The lions ran up to him, and he swirled around in a quick motion to hit the lion on the left with the sword, and puncture through its face with his knife. One down, one injered lion more to go. He took the knife and ran one side of it through his face to get the blood cleaned. He was now covered in blood – none of his own. The lion realized that his partner was now gone, and it was wounded on its stomach and left too. It was limping along, circling him, feigning away from him. The fun part is now here!

"That's enough."

Karthik turned around and saw a tall, buff man standing on the top row seat. "I've seen enough. Clean yourself up, and come to the court," he stopped speaking, frozen in terror.

Karthik immediately knew what was happening. He ducked, just to escape the lion's punch, and the lion pounced on him from behind. He stabbed it with his sword from beneath it, and they both fell down. The blood. Ah, heavenly. The blood from the lion's head chest flowed through his face, and down to the back of his head. He felt it wetting his hair. He lay there for a while, soaking in blood for a moment. He threw the lion down and laid there for some more time. He was then suddenly yanked to reality by the woman standing next to the princess, who was looking at him in absolute horror from the stand above. He stood up and walked into the gates he was called to, where there were a lot of men chained in cells. There were a lot of bunker shaped iron doors on the ground, the rooms of which could only be underground. Dungeons! There were changing rooms, he assumed were for the guards just near the cells, and the guards brought him a set of weapons, all brand-new, and a red robe to wear. He took a bath and realized what had happened in the arena was not under his control, at all. *Always be the master of your own mind. If you're driven by instincts, you're insulting the universe's gift of common sense.* He remembered his father's words. Too late. Valli had seen him for who he was. He wore the new robes and walked into the courtroom. The princess, the man from the arena, and a few others were in their seats. A few slaves, including Valli, stood around these people. The horror hadn't left her eyes yet.

"I told you, I know a gifted human when I see one, Banu" Asumugi spoke, pointing Karthik to a man who wore what seemed like a lion's mane around his neck.

"True. Sorry to have doubted your judgement, Aunt Asumugi," the man from the stairs replied. From what Karthik had heard about the royalty and their backstories, the man with the aesthetics of the lion was Singamugan, the brother of the Tarakan - the caretaker of Mount Kraunch, and the king Soorapadhman himself. The man from the stairs, as Asumugi said, would be Banukopan, the king's oldest son.

Karthik had not fully recovered from the trance he'd put himself into inside the arena and could still smell the blood of those lions on him. He never got the chance to say his prayers for those dead lions. What would he say? Thank you for letting me show my mighty prowess on your powerless selves? He was starting to feel sick.

"Well, if only I had listened to her, I'd have saved two of my beautiful lions." Singamugan walked towards Karthik and continued, "Where were all this time, son? Moorgan, why did it take us this long to find you?"

"The streets are still filled with talent, brother. The palace disconnects us from our own people."

"You're right, Asumugi. At least he reached here, eventually. As our population grows, the competition to be the best grows too, and we simply have to let the best like him beat the competition and climb up to glory by themselves," he spoke in a very polished tone.

He wore yellow silk robes to cover himself and his long nails were painted yellow too. He had yellow hair, and his moustache was large, covering almost the whole of his cheeks like that of a lion's whiskers. He was easily at least a foot taller than Karthik. He put his hands on him before he began speaking again. "But all for good, young Moorga, all for good. If we had let you take the job at the court without testing you, we'd have forever thought that you didn't deserve the glory, and just got lucky because you pounced on a poor slave. Now we know what you're capable of. Now we know that you can dance with the swords and kill like a machine. Wow, that fight. I've never seen someone stand that still and confident with my lions running at them, never after my brother. He would've loved to see the fight, too bad. Well, some other day, we'll let him see you fight again."

"Careful, brother. He's a soldier, not a specimen," Asumugi snarled.

"Yes, yes, of course, no disrespect to young Moorgan. What a fitting name." Singamugan walked around Karthik and stood beside him now, his hand over Karthik's shoulders. "What a fitting name for a fearless war machine. Moorgan." He turned Karthik around and continued, "Today, as the commander of the entire Mahendrapuri's elite army, I have decided that you are part of the Kottravai army's Maveerar platoon, the highest rank in the army after the generals. You will now wear this around your neck all the time." He put an iron chain with a pearl pendant around Karthik's neck. "This alone stays on you when you leave the palace. No information about the red robes, the palace, or anything about what lies inside the inner walls reaches anyone outside. You can continue to live outside for your work, pretending to be a peasant, but remember, you are not really a peasant anymore. You are a part of the world's best platoon, under the great Singamugan, led by the great king Soorapadhman," Singamugan proclaimed. "You have great power in your hand now." Singamugan touched the pearl with his index finger. "Which means your life isn't really yours anymore."

"Enough, brother. Leave the poor boy alone. Come with me, Moorgan. I'll brief you."

Asumugi signalled that he follow her, and walked out from one of the doors. As upset, confused, and overwhelmed as he was, Karthik still noticed how tall the ceiling was, and saw the stairs leading up to higher floors of the palace. They walked to the floor above, and Asumugi sat down on a chair at the edge of the balcony. The three women around her brought her a pouch and a drink. Valli started fanning her with a hand fan made of peacock feathers. It hurt Karthik, and he now understood why that Kurinji man had tried to kill Asumugi.

"I am sorry for the lack of…" Asumugi paused to take a sip out of her cup. The cup was made of copper too. "Decency, for the lack of a better word, in how Singamugan explained the principles of this palace. But whatever he said, is true. Almost three hundred people work in the palace, and two hundred and seventy of them are slaves. So, they don't get to cross these walls, ever. We're not worried about them. But soldiers like you, you get to come in and go back out into the city. You're one of the ways through which we, the royalty, understand how the city works. However, it is equally possible that the city might be able to see inside the palace as well, through you. That, we don't want." She took another sip. "Every day, you'll walk into the palace, stand in the courtyard, and be a part of the proceedings of the day. You see the king – mind you, not everybody in the city gets to see him. A select few, a blessed few get to see my brother, the ruler of this heaven on Earth. Every day, you see us; you even get to hear the daily deals and discussions of the government. That is too much power and information for a man from the people, Moorgan. People and government are not the same, and should never be one and the same. They should be two parallel lines, travelling along, but never touching. You'll be given a separate room in one of these barracks and you can stay there forever if you wish to. If you wish to go out, you're free to do so too, but only after leaving all of the possessions you collected from here in your room. You can take your old items from there, leave for the city, and come back to the room and get dressed before you enter the palace. The red robe stays within the bounds of the inner walls, and you'll remove it before you cross the wall. Along with it, you'll remove every piece of information you know about the palace, the government, and the royalty, and leave it in the barrack room before you leave for the city. You're no longer serving people, Moorgan. You're doing something far more important. You're serving the family of the king, and the king himself. Act accordingly. If you are found guilty, there's no trial, there's no court hearing, and there's no going back to your old life. We'll not kill you, either. The betrayers of the kingship are punished in a way that they'll spend their lives on their knees, begging for something as simple as death."

Valli could not take any more of this and dropped the tray with drinks. Asumugi turned to her and laughed. "What, the princess of Kurinji cannot handle a little horror story?"

Karthik was uncomfortable with what was happening here. He kept wishing that whatever he did helped the heist somehow.

"You may leave now, Moorgan. Stay here in the barracks if you want or leave if you want, we don't really care. But be here tomorrow, and every day after tomorrow at 8 AM sharp. Friday's are off, and you get to spend time however you want."

Asumugi turned around, and ordered the three of them to clean up the mess and bring her a new batch of wine. For one last time, before he left the room, Karthik and Valli exchanged a glance. He looked into her eyes and she, into his.

Karthik walked out of the palace and changed in one of the barrack rooms. Before walking out of the inner wall's gates, he took one good look at the palace. He saw a big man standing on the fourth-floor balcony, looking into the city. He wore a crown and was easily more than seven or seven and a half feet tall. Was he who Karthik thought he was? Was he? The infamous king of the infamous asura clan, the God of the deserts, and the proclaimer of the seas himself? Was he Soorapadhman? Well, he'd come back tomorrow to see him anyway. And every day after tomorrow. For how long, though?

Kill some bad people, Moorgan.

Chapter 14
Buying Freedom

Kadalon was sure he had looked here, thrice. She could not possibly be here. But he still wanted to look, just one more time. They had really loved sharing intimate silences and long meaningless conversations in the company of the waves. He'd really hoped to be able to get a glimpse of those deep, fathomless eyes once again, near the seashore. '*Well, not the shore exactly, but the closest one can get in this damned place*,' he thought.

He sat on the rocky beach, watching the waves crash into the pile of rocks beneath him, and the frothed water running into the crevices of the rocks. Karthik and he had split up the day before, and he was already paranoid. He appreciated the sheer silence he was able to enjoy after months, but the kid was surely a danger magnet. If he was not getting into trouble, he was making trouble. How many times did he fall off his head from the glider as a child? That must be the only reason, right?

He smiled at the thought of Karthik. As much as he complained about him, and even though every single complaint was true, the kid had heart. Something that nobody in this town seemed to have. Everybody was as lively as the bricks of the wall dividing the city. He picked up a stone and threw it into the sea. '*Where are you, Kannukkiniya*?' he thought. He reckoned it'd be easier to find the stone he just threw into the water than to find the lost love of his life in this place.

He decided to wait some more. He had nothing to do in the evening anyway. He stared at every person who roamed there, wearing a brown cloth. He noticed a black robe was walking towards him. He casually touched his face to make sure his veil was on as well. The closer the soldier came, the more he realized this was the nuisance he had ditched the day before.

"Well, I at least knew where to find you," Karthik spoke as he sat down. The sun was setting, and Karthik never grew tired of watching the sun slowly drop into the sea. "I'll just finish watching," he put his hand out when Kadalon started asking him something.

It usually wasn't as cloudy near the horizon during sunset, but that day it was. The sun sunk into the clouds and illuminated them from behind. Light and colours seemed almost as if they were spilling out of the white clouds. Layers and layers of clouds, and the sun kept dropping down, showing itself and hiding, again, and again, and again. Finally, its tip touched the horizon. The reflection crawled through the entire sea, reaching up to the shore. As if someone had drawn an orange line on an infinite blue rock bed. And it set. In minutes, Mother Nature proved everybody who called themselves artists to be simply amateurs. Karthik was tearing up. He sighed as the sun went out of sight, and turned towards Kadalon.

"What?" Kadalon asked, removing his veil.

"I have to say something, man."

Karthik had no idea how this was going to go down.

"Please don't tell me you fucked something up."

"I fucked something up, I think."

"One day, Moorgan. It has been one day since we split up."

Karthik was amazed at how well-composed Kadalon was, and how he even chose to still address him as Moorgan, even at the height of his anger.

"Look, for once, I didn't seek trouble. I just followed a series of causes and effects, and to cut a long story short, I am a royal guard now," he showed Kadalon the pearl on his neck.

"Royal what?" Kadalon stared in disbelief.

"Yea. And I think I saw Soorapadhman. And I definitely spoke to Singamugan and Banukopan and Asumugi."

Kadalon could see Karthik was totally confused about the entire thing himself, so he would listen to the full story before reacting, he resolved to himself. They walked to the chathram that Karthik was staying in, and Karthik told him about the Kottravai temple, the palace, the lions, and the rules of royalty.

"Well, at least I found Valli."

"How the hell have you not exposed the entire plan to them by now?"

"I had my backstories straight. I followed the same answers we gave at Mount Kraunch."

"But you will keep coming to the blacksmith's every Friday, right?"

"Yea. Fridays are off. I don't have to guard."

"Out of all the things you told me, the fact that all royal guards are not on duty once a day is the most useful piece of information. Incidentally, it also makes sense why the blacksmiths are so busy on Fridays. We'll meet up this one week on Friday and change it thereafter. The fact that there is a possibility of a looming royal guard is not good."

"Hey, don't talk shit about royal guards, okay," Karthik showed him the pearl and made a silly scary face behind the veil. "Also, I just told you I'm only free on Fridays and you proceed to move the meeting to some other day. What is really up with you?"

"Logically, you cannot be a part of the plans that we make hereafter. Without knowing what lies beyond the inner walls, I cannot make plans for you. So, you'll relay the information that you think will help us to Devayanai on your Friday visits, and we'll probably collect it on Saturdays. If we have anything to say to you, it'll go through Deva too, I guess. But talking to Deva a lot will get her in trouble. I'm not sure how things will work. But we'll have to do it. I can't risk our plans even after knowing royal guards are out there on the same day that we choose to have our little therapy sessions. We'll find a way out before Friday. Don't worry."

"Or, I can buy her."

"You can what?"

Karthik pulled out the yellow coin from his backpack. "Asumugi told me this is a copper coin, and it's incredibly valuable. I could probably use it to free your sister from her lord and pay the shack owner off. If I can strike a bargain, I can get him to release Deva, and spare me a thousand iron coins as well. This seems to be a novelty, really. I've seen this coin open every door in the country. I mean, not literally, but you get it, right? I didn't actually go opening all the doors with this one."

"Stop talking so much rubbish, man. We've got to focus. Talking about the buying power of this thing, if you can buy a slave AND a thousand more iron coins, why not buy the entire shack? You could restrict entry and make it private. We're the only surviving members of our legion, remember? You could justify the story by saying you gifted the lads their own shack as a token of celebration now that you've made it as a royal guard. This will even give us lot some credibility. It'll also mean a couple of more poor slaves get a good owner too," Kadalon spoke as he looked at the coin and examined it closely.

"Princess Asumugi said that this coin could buy the entire outer ring. Should we? We can set them all free?" Karthik gleamed with hope. To his knowledge, there were around 50 Kurinji folk in the outer circle alone.

"Nah, my plan will show you as an arrogant, lavish soldier who respects his roots and mates. Your plan will show you as a compassionate man setting slaves free. Governments don't like the compassionate ones, especially if compassion gets in the way of their plan of keeping people divided. We need you in a very strong position inside the inner walls. So, for now, we're buying the shack."

"Sure. Do I inform this to the people in the castle?"

"Don't just inform. Gloat. Thank the people for giving you an opportunity to celebrate. Live up to the role of a Palai soldier. They all have big egos."

"Nice. You never really told me. Why do you spend so much time on the rock beach? Because you feel at home?"

"Something like that," Kadalon sighed. His plan had taken a few sharp turns that day. A lot of new things to consider. Kadalon stayed with Karthik that night. The next morning, Karthik woke him up to tell him that he was leaving for work. He knew that in a day or two, Deva would be freed. Not technically, but she would be, yes.

One or maybe more slaves would be freed too. Who knew how many more to go? Was Kannukkiniya inside the castle too?

Chapter 15

Red, Black, Blue, and Brown

He'd woken up early that day. He spent more time than usual praying. The lingam in the room next to his office stood as a testimony to the elaborate rituals he'd performed that morning. He'd done his yoga. He was bathed, dressed, and standing on his balcony for some time now. After prayers and art, people-watching was the most soothing activity for him.

The town clearly seemed industrious. The blue sea expanse and his tiny spec of a city amidst it was his world. People roamed around, doing their jobs meticulously, mostly dressed in white. The black-robed guards were stationed to protect them and the brown-clothed people. This was all he cared about. The symmetry of the city was impeccable. Indeed, Asumugi was the greatest artist he'd seen.

He really felt that he should be there, among the people. But there had been multiple attempts of assassination. So, over the years, they'd separated themselves from the rest of the crowd. He was made aware of the recent happenings at the Kottravai temple too. He liked to keep it professional and calm. He assured everyone that it was nothing and that he'd double up the protection for every royalty member. He'd even sent a message to Tarakan to keep himself safe. He was a fool. He would have to be kept an eye on.

The winds carried the smell of sea and confusion. He really did not know what to do. What if something happened to this beautiful city? What if something happened to his family? His people?

"Father?"

"Banukopan, my son." He picked up his fallen heart and held his chin high. "Let you have all the wealth in the world, and let you live a long, healthy, and happy life," he blessed Banukopan.

"Thank you, father. I've come to inform you that the court proceedings are about to start."

"I will be there, you go on."

He needed a minute. As Banukopan walked out, he knelt in front of the lingam, and once again prayed that the blessings he gave his son came true. He picked up a handful of vibhoothi, the holy ash, and smeared it on his forehead.

He walked down and the court stood up. He hated it when they did that. He signalled for the people to sit. A young soldier walked up front and put his hands together in a traditional greeting.

"Let your valour serve Mahendrapuri, and let your name be feared by foes," he blessed.

"Ayya, my name is Moorgan. I have been asked to join the Maveerar platoon. I thought it only fair that I introduce myself to you," the boy spoke loud and clear.

"Moorgan, as the ruler and protector of Mahendrapuri, I welcome you to the most elite, most courageous, and the most loyal army platoon in the entire peninsula. And as a brother, I'm eternally grateful to you."

"I'm humbled, ayya." The boy greeted him again and stepped into the backdrop.

There were twelve soldiers in the courtroom – each one standing near one of the pillars of the big room. He awkwardly stood in between a couple of pillars, with his back against the wall. He held the spear a bit wonky and stood with his weight on one of his legs.

"Singa, agenda?" he asked.

Asumugi walked in with her three slaves. "You're late."

"Sorry, my king."

She immediately noticed Moorgan in the hall. Even with the red robe and veil, his lethargic stance and small frame gave him away. She nodded in approval as he recognized her, even with silk veil on. She laughed at his goofy position in her perfectly symmetrically set up courtroom.

"Singa?" Soorapadhman asked again.

"We have a couple of visitors as a part of the foreign policy. They're here to deposit some iron. We're shipping salt and the statues that they ordered. I have asked them to stay at the second ring guest-house. I don't think there should be anything important, but they did ask to meet you."

"Maybe in the evening, in my spare time."

"Yes, my king. I shall inform them. Apart from that, all we have left is our own town's petitions, which we received from our elders when we met them last evening. Most of them enquired about the well-being of Princess Asumugi, so we might have to parade her just to boost up people's morale. The folks from the Yaazhi sheds all over the city have requested a little more help and have asked for more slaves. Our recent attack was from slave from the Yaazhi camps. Might have been because he was overworked. We have a few requests for better roads, and the places without clean water fountains have requested that we fix them. There were a dozen more simpler requests, but I'm sure Prince Banukopan has dealt with them and delegated the one-offs to the respective authorities."

"Arriving," the guard at the entrance called out, loud and clear. The echo filled the entire courtroom. "Arriving, arriving. The king of the mountain, the keeper of our mighty gates, and the protector of Mahendrapuri, the valiant, the fearsome, and the fiercest commander on all of the peninsula, Chief Tarakasuran, arriving, arriving, arriving."

A big man stood at the courtroom entrance, staring at the guard. "Next time, just fucking say my name first and let it be. You just wasted the entire court's time," Tarakan put his hands out and sighed. "We all know who we all are. The introductions are for when we meet the public or in front of those pesky foreign rats."

"Tarakaa," Singamugan exclaimed and ran towards him. His big frame running seemed like an odd sight, but the grace made it look natural.

"Brother," Tarakan wished him with his hands together and embraced him.

Though Karthik had entered through the Mount Kraunch gate and had been, in fact, quarantined there for three days, he'd never once seen the great king of the mountain, Tarakasuran. What was with this family's height? They were all giants, towering casually over six and a half or seven feet. Tarakan was much darker in complexion compared to his siblings Soorapadhman and Singamugan. He wore bones for a chain and no jewellery whatsoever, other than the bones. He had ashes smeared on his forehead, hands, and elbows. After greeting Singamugan, Tarakan bowed down to greet Soorapadhman, still on his throne. "My king."

"Commander," Soorapadhman nodded formally. "I assume you're here because of the note I sent earlier?"

"Yes, my king. Despite multiple attempts, I wanted to know why the princess would be so reckless."

"Enough, Tarakan. Let's discuss family in our free time. Do not waste the court's time," Asumugi said, still poised on her throne.

"Well, now I'm just disappointed that the mercenary did not do his job properly."

"Tarakaa," Soorapadhman shouted, and both Asumugi and Tarakasuran dropped their heads. "Asumugi, you have to understand that the life of royalty is not a matter of family alone. We are answerable to the entire city. Today, one guy decided to rebel. Imagine if a thousand slaves rebel tomorrow? Of course, every soldier of mine will slay them like rag dolls and feed them to the fierce ocean, but at what cost? At what cost are going to fend them off? I do not want bloodshed from my people. With all this violence, with all these people uprooted from their villages and settlements, and with the tensions running high, we need to do something about this. And until we do something to ensure that there will be no more uproar, we will have to brace for smaller attacks like this one, springing up here and there. More importantly, we will have to prioritize saving ourselves and our people from this... vengeance."

"I say we execute that filthy rat. We execute him in the middle of the city. We rip his arms off for raising a weapon against royalty, we gauge his eyes for looking our sister straight in the eye and deciding to kill her, and we hang his bleeding body to rot and die, tied to a tree. We take this chance and send a warning. I say we kill that filthy rat dead and feed him to seagulls," Tarakan replied.

"No. That'll just feed into more aggression. For now, nobody really knows what happens inside the inner walls. The dungeons are filled with terrorists like him, and that'll continue. In a few months, he'll grow tired and demented from the loneliness and darkness, so much so that he'll want to scoop Yaazhi poop for time pass," Asumugi said, and her voice sent shivers down Karthik's spine. He feared Asumugi's beauty and the sultry voice more than all her three brothers combined. He saw her glancing at his side and met her in the eye. "And if I did go outside, and if people did spring up on me with a knife, we have heroes who can save me."

"No, you are not going anywhere. Neither is anyone else from the royalty. I will personally arrange a parade, and we shall address the people of the town, or at least meet them. Only after I've examined the situation and city thoroughly, though. Don't be reckless, Asumugi."

"And what are you going to do when I go to the beach after court? Tie me up in the dungeon? Don't be paranoid, Singa. We're a clan of warriors. It's nauseating to think we've become the pretentious people who don't want to deal with sweat, blood, and mud. If I weren't praying, I'd have killed the fool myself, you know?" Asumugi put her hand out for a drink and one of the three slaves gave her a glass while another poured her a drink.

"Since when are we drinking in court?" Tarakan threw his hands in the air.

"It's just grape juice. Shut up and leave, Tarakana. I'm fine."

"Yes, yes, you are, and if not for Moorgan, we'd be scraping your blood out from the floors of Kottravai temple," Singamugan exclaimed.

Asumugi rolled her eyes and continued sipping out of the glass. Soorapadhman just sat there, distracted.

"My king?" Banukopan called. "The city is growing restless by the day, my king. The slave neighbourhoods are getting too populous. There are more quarrels every day among the different clans. Sometimes, even different settlements of the same clan have fights. There have been a few instances of people trying to escape the high walls or even through the docks. Our soldiers guarding Mount Kraunch brought them to justice. I understand that you mean good by bringing in more slaves, but where do we accommodate them? Also, when do we stop? There are half as many slaves as there are citizens of the Palai clan. We need you to do something about this."

"The court is no place to be emotional, my brotheren," he stood up and was still for a while. "Yet," he continued, and by now he'd started pacing in front of the throne, "and yet, all of you make it so hard for me not TO KILL EVERY SINGLE ONE OF YOU, RIGHT HERE," he screamed out of nowhere. "We're not executing slaves, we're not provoking them any further, and we're waiting until it's a good time to venture out again, and we ARE worried about our sister, yes. But we're not kids trying to insult or outsmart each other. We're grown adults, and we're in a courtroom. So, first of all, stop fucking drinking in court, and second, stop leaving the mountain unguarded. Tarakan, go back to the fucking mountain. Singamugan, prepare our soldiers for unexpected attacks like this, but do it subtly, under the covers. And you, Asumugi, my dear fucking sister, you're not going anywhere for at least a week. And if possible, lose your exotic collection of," he fanned his hands in haste towards the three people behind her, "stewardesses. For fuck's sake, let's keep it professional in the court. We're not running a summer camp here, no. Thousands of lives depend on us. Hundreds of people trust us with their lives. Let's not gamble with that. Clear?"

Asumugi, Tarakasuran and Singamugan nodded in unison. "Good."

He stormed out of the court and vanished into the big drapes separating the courtroom from the rest of the palace.

"Moorgan, come with me. You three, get lost," Asumugi stormed. Karthik, suddenly brought to reality, ran after her.

"Where the hell do you think you're going?" Singamugan asked.

"To the beach."

Karthik wondered if he should go. He decided it'd be wise to stay in Asumugi's good books, considering she was the one who made it possible for him to work there. God, it had been one day, and he was already being sucked into the politics between power centres. This is why he chose the nomad life, he sighed as he jogged to catch up with Asumugi. He greeted both the brothers before he ran past their line of sight, beyond the court hall's drapes.

Chapter 16

Mortals, Mother Kottravai and the Muni's Return

"You should listen to your brother," Karthik said, breaking a long silence.

"My brother is your king. I'd prefer if you addressed him that way."

"In that case, you should listen to our king."

"Your king is my brother. I own these lands. I cannot be told what to do."

"Well, I should've stuck to listening to the waves crash."

Asumugi laughed. He turned back towards the sea. Karthik was in his black robe, and Asumugi, though a little underdressed for royalty, definitely looked fancier than everyone on the beach. Her face was covered and she was wearing black as well. The pearl waist chain she donned, showed itself in a brighter shade in contrast to her black dress.

"You'll get used to our proceedings."

"That is how the court proceeds?" He bit his tongue. Maybe it wasn't wise to speak shit about his employer.

"A little more civilized in front of outsiders. But pretty much like this always, yes."

"They have a point. It is unwise to put one's life in jeopardy for a beach view."

"For this view, I'd die."

"That you are right about."

Karthik sat down to simply do what he did best. Stare into the void.

"Do you visit the temple often?"

"Mother Kottravai's? Yes." And then he remembered, "I really wish I had your talent, though. What a masterpiece it is, the idol that's sitting there in the temple."

"I have always believed that Mother Kottravai liked to be a lot fiercer than how these men want her to look. I first sculpted an idol that had no clothes covering her, with human guts all around her shoulders. There was a beheaded body lying beneath her legs, and a head in one of her hands, just like now. The priests were shocked, and wanted me to make another one, a little less… what's the word, intimidating. She is the Goddess of wrath, after all."

"Certainly would have given the temple a little eeriness, that one. However, it would've been one hell of an art piece."

"It is. It sits in the basement. In the coffers. They'd not even have it in the sculpture warehouse."

"Why? It surely belongs somewhere in the city."

"People don't want to see Gods that are fierce and strict, Moorgan. People want a forgiving God. Pleasant faces, peaceful eyes, easy to please with just words and art. People do not want a God that judges and serves justice, just one that guides and preaches. So, a violent Goddess is not accepted, even if the man she killed supposedly represented all evil against women."

"I don't think it's that deep. I think people simply tend to shy away from morbidity."

"That's an easy way out of the argument."

"I don't know, but I say it again. There's some place for it, surely."

"Thanks."

'*So, it happened,*' Karthik thought as he rode his Yaazhi back to his place. He'd informed Singamugan about his decision to buy the forge. Singamugan hugged him and said if every soldier had a bit of this spirit, Mahendrapuri would live forever. Yet, he was upset that Asumugi had blatantly disobeyed the king's court order.

"At least she took you with her; we were a bit relieved she had someone protecting her," he'd said.

Karthik realized how deep he'd got into the lives of the royalty in just a matter of days. It had been one day, after all. He was tired after a long day of work. He knew a food joint where they served delicious deer meat, something he loved to bits, something that was too rare and costly in the city. Understandably so.

He bought his Yaazhi a chunk of fresh leaves in the market and left him in a shelter, instructing the keeper not to chain him. He then walked to the chathram, the food place. He sat to eat and got down to business. In the middle of his meal, he noticed someone come and sit next to him.

"Moorgan, new work, eh?"

"How did you get in here? We're in the second layer, how do you even have access here?"

It was the short muni again. Agathiyan.

"Ah, you know me, you know me. I'm everywhere, going to all sorts of places, doing my own things. It's not about me today, it's about you! Celebrating your new job with a little treat to yourself, I assume?"

The sadhu took off the towel draped around his neck and laid it down next to him. "A little fish curry and *thinai* for me, please? If you could add a little salt to it, oh, I'd love it!"

"So, you can afford salt now? I thought you were a beggar?"

"I get by, yes, yes I do. It's because people like me can afford salt that the empire of Mahendrapuri stands this tall, Moorgan."

"What?"

"Do you know about this place? The man who today stands towering over the palace of this wonderful city was once picking up salt on the hot beaches of Tiruchendhur."

"It's ruled by the kings. Wait, is it safe to talk about all this here? I don't wanna blow my cover."

"What cover? You are a soldier of Mahendrapuri, and I'm a nomad, beggar, looking to get some good food. While at it, we discuss the magnificence of this city. What cover? Why unsafe?" The muni started mixing his pudding and curry together.

"How do you know I'm a soldier?"

"You're in a black robe, Moorgan. Also, we saw it before you entered Mount Kraunch. Your lack of memory gives me migraines. Why do you love dabbling in such frivolous tasks? Frivolous, frivolous, I say. I attempt to tell him important pieces of history and he keeps trying to make the same point over and over again. Child. Child of all sorts. Look, do you want to hear what I have to say or not? If not for the tasty food, I would storm right out. I am flustered." The muni shoved some food into his mouth.

"Even when flustered your appetite seems to be fine."

The muni stopped eating and looked up, his mouth full of food. He laughed and spoke with some food still in his mouth, "A man must eat, you know."

"So let's eat, and go back to my cottage. My Yaazhi will be happy to see you, and my humble abode will be blessed with your wisdom."

The muni smiled and continued ploughing through the fish and rice. The salt tasted incredibly good. At what cost though? The food wasn't any less tasty given the amount of blood in it.

"Oh, we are going to a cottage alright, but not yours. We're going to someone else's cottage. One with a lot of hoarded gooseberries. Oh, what wonderful gooseberries they are..." and the muni continued to spend a solid five minutes talking about gooseberries. '*What awaited in this gooseberry cottage now?*' Karthik thought with a sigh.

"Agathiyaa, welcome to my abode."

They were now in the third layer, the one filled with teachers and merchants. This particular cottage, an isolated one, located amidst unusually thick vegetation for a city like Mahendrapuri, was just as big as his room. The entire front wall, however, had been taken down and white cowhide was hung on the back wall.

"And Moorgan, child, how long we all have been waiting!"

An old woman welcomed them both and hugged Karthik. She smelled of vibhooti, honey, and divinity. "Welcome, welcome," she kissed him on his forehead. She had no teeth, whatsoever, and Karthik was a little embarrassed, but this was the first forehead kiss he'd got since his last day at home. His mom had sent him off on his adventure with a forehead kiss, so he accepted it with little grace and a lot of nostalgia.

"I'm Avvai!" She kissed him again before letting him go. She rushed into the next room and reappeared a couple of minutes later.

"Here." She looked around as she dropped a handful of gooseberries into Karthik's hand. "Keep them with you, yea. These are for you. If this man or anyone asks you for any, don't share. These are for you, from this old grandma. Are you eating at all? You don't look as fit, Moorgan. Royal guard or not, you must eat a lot. Come, let's eat. You must be hungry."

"No, no, amma. We just ate."

"Che, I'm too old to be your amma. Call me aachi. I'm easily a grandmother. Also, you, Agathiyan, you knew you were coming here, yet you come after a hefty meal? How am I to feed my child now? You spoil him with chathram food. The water they use is not healthy, Moorgan. The more you eat home-cooked food, the better your shape will become. You're a little skinny. Wait, I'll prepare something for you to eat."

"We're not hungry, Mother Avvai, really," Agathiyan replied.

"So, you'll not eat here? Okay, I see how it is. Grown-up people you all are. Eating in chathrams and chaavadis, salt and other delicacies. Why would you want an old fart's meal?" she sighed. "Do you people at least want some mangoes?"

This was the first time Karthik saw a woman with no teeth talk. It was so funny to him. I mean, her mouth was basically moving non-stop.

"Amma, if you don't mind, I'd like to know why we're here," Karthik requested. He saw a bunch of birds randomly come into the abode and carry away some millets kept in one corner of the house. "Also, birds are stealing your food. Shoo."

"Hello, hello, why are you rude to my birds? They'll go poop all over your Yaazhi if you're too rude," Avvai laughed.

"Oh sorry, are they yours?"

"Well, is the Yaazhi yours?"

Karthik understood. "Also, did he eat? The Yaazhi?" She peeped outside the walls to see the big animal swaying and testing grounds, in front of her gurukulam. "What's his name? Handsome fellow, he is! Just like our Muni here."

"Oh, you called me handsome. I think you have a little skewered perception of what's beautiful, Mother Avvai." Agathiyan spoke.

"Ayo, I never lie. You are beautiful, you look like a cute kozhukattai." She pulled Agathiyan's beard playfully. "Hey, did your Yaazhi eat?" she glared at Karthik, and he nodded. "Oh well," she sighed as she got up, picked up a big watermelon from the next room, and waddled towards the Yaazhi. By now, Karthik was convinced that she was just another person who was seeing things and speaking to inanimate objects, like the muni himself. He sighed. What was he doing with his life anyway?

"Don't disregard Mother Avvai's intelligence because she's innocent, Karthikeya. She knows the entire world like it's the back of her hand," the muni said as if answering the questions on Karthik's mind while munching on a gooseberry. "Gooseberry?"

"Ayya, I'm on the edge of my sanity. I've come to a foreign land to honour a dead man's promise, and I've inadvertently been recruited into one of the most elite platoons where everybody is simply a foot taller than me. The girl I've been searching for over a year is serving wine to the princess, and there are hungry eyes everywhere I look in this town. There are slaves that look at me like it's somehow my fault that they're here in shackles. I cannot deal with any more of this clownery. Just, just tell me what I must do."

"See, this is the question you should've been asking all along. What and not the why or how!" the muni exclaimed. But he quickly realized and put his hand on Karthik's shoulder. "It's okay, Karthikeya. Things can only get better from here. There's not much room for entropy."

"Don't tempt fate, Agathiyan," Avvai came back with Karthik's spear. "Sweet, sweet fellow that guy outside is. It is a crime that he has no name. I have decided to call him Pillaiyaar, for the sweet child he is."

She shook her hips in a little excitement and did a little dance. If it wasn't for the million questions in his head, Karthik would've laughed so much. She was such a cute old lady. Round and squishy, her skin a little wrinkled. *How does this woman eat? She has no teeth.* Karthik smiled at the silly thought.

"Well, it takes a while for me to eat. I usually keep food in my mouth for a couple of minutes, until it softens. Also, my gums have got a little stronger over the years; I chew with them. Eeeee," she smiled, showing her toothless mouth.

"Oh, I give up," Karthik sighed.

"Okay, the last question before my children come in for the shift. How old are you? Have you turned twenty-one yet?" Avvai asked.

"I have lost count of the years I've been away from my home. When I left, I was almost thirteen."

"And it's been eight years since he started travelling, so yea. He's somewhere around twenty-one," the muni answered, his mouth so full of gooseberries.

"Che, who taught you manners? Talking with so much food in the mouth. Did you give him your gooseberries?" Avvai asked Karthik. Karthik shook his head. "Good." She turned to Agathiyan and asked, "Hello, are you stealing gooseberries?" Agathiyan nodded a yes. "Some muni you are. Always stealing food. Okay, you both help me clear the area. I have a bunch of children coming in for their evening classes in about ten minutes."

Karthik and the muni cleared the room. Mostly it was simply scattered fruits, dry leaves, and bird feed.

It was late in the evening and starting to get dark. Avvai slowly moved around the house, oiling lamps and lighting them up, one after another. Gradually, he saw children of different ages come in groups and sit in the abode. They sat facing the animal skin on the wall, and Avvai started attending to them. In a while, the place was full of children dressed in brown clothing, and Avvai was speaking to them all. Karthik, though had no business being there, was still waiting for two old people to explain things to him.

"Hello Agaliga, running nose, eh? Ask your mother to prepare a Tulsi-Homam broth. Now everybody, what was yesterday's class about?"

"*Kadivadhu Mara,*" the students sang in unison.

"Very nice, very good," Avvai clapped. "Oi, Maara, stand. Tell me, what does it mean?"

"You shouldn't be angry all the time. Anger isn't good for you."

"Good. Now, is it good for us to hit our younger brother?"

"No." The boy looked down to his right, to his brother. "Sorry."

"Aha, nice. Now children, today, we learn that the greatest form of spirituality or virtue is to save another life from trouble. Repeat after me, *Kaappathu Viradham,*

Kaapadhu Viradham."

Ironically, Karthik started listening and found himself agreeing with most of what Avvai taught. In an hour or so, Avvai wrapped the session up and instructed Agaliga once again to have the broth as she was leaving. Once the children left, she came to Karthik, touched his head, and ran her fingers through his hair. "How good of a child you are. No oil in hair though. Bloody rough it is."

"Mother Avvai, I must leave," the muni stood up. Karthik stood up with him too, ready to leave for his place. "No, you stay here, assist her to feed the animals," he said. Karthik agreed. At this point, he was still mulling over the concepts he'd heard in the class she took for the children, and did not know how to process half that information.

"Do you have someplace to be, Agathiyan? It is already late. I'm sure your errands can wait until morning. You can leave after breakfast."

The muni showed no sign of resistance and sat down immediately.

"Karthikeya," the old woman stood up, her voice a little clearer and louder than before, engulfing all of Karthik's attention. "The son of all that is and all that will be, you have been given the honour of saving these people, and putting an end to this violent way of life. From Agathiyan, from your face, and from simply how things are, I learn that you have a lot of doubts about yourself, and more so, about the nature of reality itself. I will explain to you why it is important for you to trust yourself. To trust the process. To trust the very nature of being itself. Karthikeya, for that, I must tell you the story of how this peninsula was before things went sour. I must tell you about the greatest civilization yet to live on the face of this round planet. I, Avvai, the daughter of Thamizh itself, will tell you the story of the great Thamizh civilization, and how Mahendrapuri came to be. This wretched, cursed way of living is cancer on the land, Karthikeya. You will cut the tumour out of this land, and pave way for a better path of living. That is your destiny, and you will do exactly that."

Chapter 17
The Clan of Gods

"An eternity ago, man could not even dream of having all that he has today. He wasn't what he is today, the king of this place. He didn't tower over the beasts of nature like he does today. Before stones became weapons, before the fire became our friend, man was simply a slave to the very nature of his animal self, simply scraping bones to eat for a living, and climbing on top of trees at night, fearing for his life. A lot of miracles took place to help him get to where he is now. One of the most profound miracles was when he learnt how to communicate better than the other beasts around him. The gift of language itself helped him relay information faster and store it for generations to come. The clans that spoke first became the Gods that we pray to today. The Thamizh clan, our clan, was among the first to open up to the possibility of developing a full-fledged, functioning language. A gift given to us by the great munis, bearers of all knowledge thus forth, and the direct descendants of Aadhi himself – the first sentient man.

They pushed the limits of the human intellect, made a million words, assigned meanings, and taught us all about it, so we thrived. The Thamizh clan – the people who spoke Thamizh – split up as we grew and travelled to the far sides of the peninsula. To the mountains, plateaus, seas, forests, and deserts. Each of these divisions named itself after the geography they chose to settle in. You already know two of them, the people of the Kurinji clan or the mountains, and the people of Neidhal clan or the sea. Then, there was the Mullai clan, the people of the forests; the Marudham clan, people of plateaus, and finally, the Palai clan, people of the deserts.

The first ones to settle were the people who took the mountains and forests, areas that offered sustenance without much effort. Their valiance and courage to endure the harshest of living conditions were rewarded with abundant sources of food and water. Then, people settled alongside the shores of the sea, where the sea fed them, kept them occupied, and provided them with livelihood. As agriculture and domestication of plants became increasingly possible, a sect of the people who were left set out to till the land, water it, alter its composition, sow seeds, take care of it, and produce food for themselves. These were the people of Marudham. Each of these clans or sects were thriving, making use of Mother Nature's gift to them. They toiled hard to make a living, and provide for everybody around them. Thus, we became the first people to settle down and make peace with Mother Nature herself, instead of wandering around, gathering whatever was in our way. We taught the world that there was a better way of life than simply being nomads. We were the clan that people wished to be, learn from, and looked up to.

The munis helped us settle, taught us the ways of life, and educated our children for a better tomorrow. Our legacy grew and each clan produced more. We shared, prospered, and taught each other our ways of life. We grew together as one with just one powerful tool in our hand – our ability to communicate, our language, Mother Thamizh herself. We were the Thamizh Kudi, spread all over the peninsula. Two hundred years ago, they first made contact. People from a foreign land, people from civilization just as advanced as ours. The people of Neidhal were the first ones to see them sail towards our land. They came from a land of sand, these people from a very faraway land, a land that had only death, destruction, and gruesome living conditions to offer. They had very few resources to survive on and a lot of people to share them with, hence they started sailing to different parts of the world. They were the bravest of explorers, for before them, nobody had ventured so far out into the sea. They spoke a language different from ours, one in which they didn't just speak, but also etched."

She pulled the animal hide on the wall down, and in the dim lights of all the lamps put together, Karthik saw symbols.

"They brought with them a cursed secret. One that the majestic Mahendrapuri stands upon. You see, Moorgan, we worshipped every form that Mother Nature took – mountains, seas, forests, and plants. Mother Nature gave us what we needed to live. We simply listened and respected our town elders. They worshipped them. The odd concept of worshipping fellow humans, the power it gave the ones at the top, the corruption it led to, the hunger it created, and their search for more power, and the responsibility vested with them justified their irrational feeling of being above the rest of the people. They came here to merely trade and look for essentials. The people of Neidhal educated them about salt and how to use it to preserve whatever scarce food they got in their cursed deserts. Though they learnt how to extract salt from the seas, they took boatloads of it whenever they came again; which they did very often. They paid heavy prices and wanted to make a deal. A deal that only the most wretched of us took."

She started coughing a little and drank some water. She coughed again and continued,

"You know something, Karthikeya? Knowledge is like the fire in the lamps here. You keep it in a pot, close it, and guard it, it dies with you. That does not mean the fire itself has died. It just means your lamp has died down, but there's always fire brewing elsewhere. Mahendrapuri, with or without us revolting against it, will fall eventually. That's simply how things are. However, if we let this man take clans and settlements into his collections of slaves, one village after another, we are simply depleting the children of Thamizh of their beautiful, valuable lives."

She coughed a little more.

"Mother Avvai, you have to rest. Karthik isn't going anytime soon, so you can continue whenever you want."

"Oh, old age is a curse, Agathiyan. You're getting there, aren't you? You'll realize. I've met the reason for my existence; my God has given me back a grandson after years. I'm spilling everything that has been bothering me all this while, and this stupid cough won't let me speak."

She couldn't control it now. She coughed and coughed and kept going. Karthik stood up, walked up to her, and refilled the water in her jug.

"Avvai Aachi, please rest. You've been talking for more than four hours straight. To the students, to ayya Agathiyan, and me. You need to rest and continue later."

"Later when? You have work tomorrow, no?" She sulked and turned away from Karthik. Karthik found it funny that she made even funnier faces with her toothless mouth.

"Aachi, I guess you're finding it difficult to manage the classes on your own. I will come here every day to help you, and you can then talk to me as much as you want. Although I must be entirely honest here, you speak a lot of things that don't make sense to me. You and him, both," he said, pointing towards the muni. "Even if I come to terms with the fact that it is my destiny to do something to help all the people enslaved here, I cannot come to terms with the fact that this has all been destined by some force of nature, even before my birth. I simply do not believe in stories like this. Although, having spent a few months here in this city, I cannot bring myself to enjoy this beautiful city after learning that all of what's here is built with the blood, sweat, and tears of innocent people who were exploited against their will."

"Why do you care, Karthikeya?" Avvai asked, stroking his hair.

"I do not know."

"Because the ones who care enough about a life other than theirs in the same way they do about theirs, are all the children of God. You, quite literally, are the child of a God."

Karthik distractedly noticed the linga in the room nearby, sitting in the middle of a bunch of flowers. He had nothing to say. He didn't understand anything, and the more he thought about the things he couldn't correlate to, the angrier he got. Was his free will a joke then? What the fuck was this place anyway? What kind of a God would let thousands of innocent souls suffer? He gave up thinking and stood.

"I'm going to have to leave, Aachi. Ayya, I assume you won't be staying any longer than tonight?"

"Actually, I'm leaving right now as well. Can I have a lift till the port?"

"Sure," he sighed, touched Avvai's feet, and walked to his Yaazhi. He noticed the Yaazhi was playing with a deer nearby. The deer ran away as soon as he stepped outside the hut. The Yaazhi bent down to let Agathiyan climb first and Karthik followed him atop the Yaazhi. They left the place, and Karthik noticed Avvai standing outside the abode, watching them leave.

"Who is she?"

"She, for all intends and purposes, is the godmother of Kannaayiran, the late leader of the Kottravai clan."

"Why does that name sound familiar?"

"Oh Moorgan, do you not remember the lies you told to enter this place?"

"Oh. Kannaayiran, Moorgan's father?"

"Yes. You see, Karthik or Moorgan, or whoever you are. You're not alone here. Even in your most private moments, even in the loneliest of walks you have, you're always accompanied. If you're pure enough to deserve it, anyway. He accompanies you everywhere, does whatever helps you in your endeavours, and guides you by the finger."

"He? Who?"

The muni lifted his hands, with this index now pointing to the sky.

"We're all here just to find out who, oh Karthikeya."

The muni and Karthik swayed as the Yaazhi walked with them on top.

"You and your bloody cryptic remarks. I wish I could simply get on the ferry with you and be done with all this bullshit."

He bit his tongue as soon as he said it. Chief Nambi. His promise. He wouldn't let him down.

"If you were able to do it and live life freely after that, there wouldn't really be any difference between you and the asuras, Karthikeya. You are who you are because of what morals you guide yourself with."

"I'm just a nomad. I liked being that way."

"Well, as a soldier of the Maveerar platoon, you're not a nomad anymore. The hopes and dreams of these sleeping souls and the justice they deserve are on your shoulders."

"Can I ask you something?"

"Yes, and I'll try and answer it as honestly as I can. Do not ask me about Mother Avvai's age, though. I do not know. She's quite old, you know, none of whom I know have seen her in her young ag…"

"No, Ayya. Not about her age. The muni clan, how many of you are in it?"

"Well, you know, unlike other clans, we do not have a settlement or flag or family. When it's time, we simply have our disciples, and we give our name to them and be done with it. So, the strength of the muni clan has always been limited. I do not know the exact count, but it was simply a handful."

"So, there was an Agathiyan before you?"

"Yes. And there will be one after me."

"Have you found the disciple?"

"My teacher didn't find or choose me, Karthikeya. I found him. That's how it works."

"And what exactly is it you do?"

"We are simply messengers. We carry messages to all the parts we can reach and deliver them. The knowledge and information that we've gathered through the years of muni lineage, we share with everyone. I, personally, for example, among many other things, have taken up the challenge of spreading the benefits of using salt in food. I learnt it long ago from the people of Neidhal, when there were still some free villages. Though it wouldn't be of any help if this city kept harbouring salt for royalty only; I think people around the world need to know more about how good of a preservative salt really is. It would really help a lot of families preserve food better, and I believe people will starve less in cold winters. A friend of mine specialized in medicinal plants, and there's one who helps people in the art of chiselling stones into weapons. Oh, how much he loves metals, you know? He's the best blacksmith I've seen. A lot of us, on personal interest, take a lot of information from one place to another. We amass knowledge and share it among civilizations."

"So essentially, you're doing the exact opposite of what Mahendrapuri is doing."

"No, Karthikeya. Mahendrapuri is doing the exact opposite of what all of humanity should be doing. They hoard instead of sharing. They oppress instead of love. And they exploit instead of helping. That's why their way of life should be damned."

"And I'm destined to do that?"

"Again, Karthikeya, destinies do not choose people. People choose a destiny."

"Just when I thought I was beginning to understand you…"

"We reached where we set out to reach!" the muni interrupted.

"Ayya, when will I be seeing you again?"

"Not anytime soon, Moorgan. I came here to bring Mother Avvai her beloved grandson. I have. So, I might not have anything better to do in this wretched town for a while. However, if you need me, I hope to be at your service."

They'd got down from the Yaazhi. The call for the last ferry to the shore was given out loud.

"Ayya, I hope I'm able to honour my promise to chief Nambi. Guide me to the truth," Karthik held his hands together and genuinely pleaded.

"Moorgan, you have prayed! *Asathoma Sathgamaya* is what all of us ask for, and I'm sure you will be answered as well. I pray for you too, my beloved child."

Karthik had heard the dialect somwhere. *Sathya* meant truth. It wasn't Thamizh. No. What was it? He'd heard this dialect elsewhere, way north of the peninsula. How did the muni speak it so fluently?

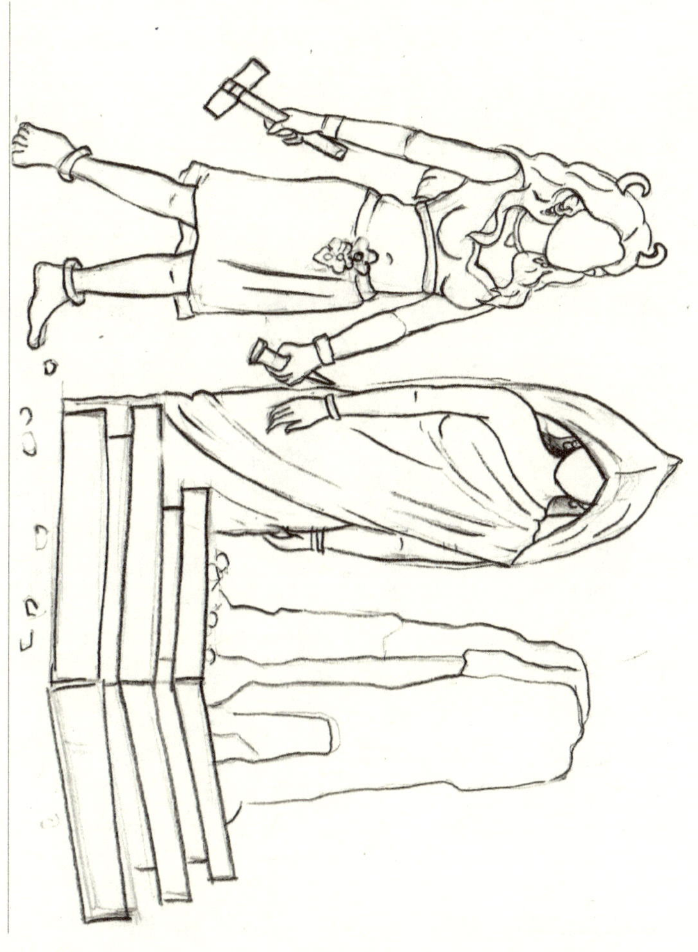

Chapter 18

Mystery Statue, Mindful Ignorance and Meticulous Plans

At the palace, Asumugi was just getting started. She finally picked one that was a couple of feet tall and had it brought to the stone table.

"You know him, don't you?" Asumugi asked Valli.

"Huh," Valli genuinely didn't know what she was talking about.

"Moorgan."

The princess started measuring portions of the stone. She had to make sure she had the proportions right. "Well, whatever happens, happens."

She picked the chisel and hammer, put them on one side of the stone, and gave it a whack. "You know him from somewhere before?"

"Uh, no." Valli decided it wasn't a very bright thing to do. Admitting to her mistress that she used to have a thing for the guy who had saved her life, and was currently flirting with this woman just as much as he did with her. Nope, not today. She wasn't ready for that kind of energy, no.

"Then why do you jump every time you see him?"

"Uh…"

"It's okay. Do you wanna know what I'm planning to do with this stone?"

"Yes, if you want to, you can share."

"I could keep it a suspense and let you figure it out as it grows. Is that what you're saying I can otherwise do? Yea, I can do that."

Oooooh, Valli liked this! This was the first time Asumugi was having any kind of non-demanding interaction with her. She wasn't a princess, not at that moment. She was simply a sculptor eager to show her work off. To know how credible her work turns out, after all the hours she'd put into punching rocks with enchanted tools. People believed these enchanted tools gave her the power to bring stones to life. They sure looked like they were alive and watching you with an eerie stillness. Valli did not believe that the tools alone were responsible for whatever came out of the stone. Asumugi was a true artist. It was hard to appreciate her for the person she was, but it was hard not to for the artist she was. The precise amount of pressure and impeccable concentration she had as the idols came near to finishing was something she hadn't seen in anyone else. It almost looked like the woman was possessed, her eyes full of light. Sometimes her eyes would be simply inches away from the chisel when she hammers it. The uli and suthi brought out a side of Asumugi that very few people had seen.

"So, you're telling me that you really don't know this guy from somewhere before? He stares at you differently as well."

No, he doesn't. Valli was fuming that he was not even breathing in the general directions of where she was in the court or anywhere else. This woman was so full of lies.

"No, he does not. He doesn't even look at anybody besides you and the king."

Asumugi turned around to look at Valli's face, simply sulking. She was intelligent. Unlike the other two, Valli's tribe was a little more communicative. They knew how to express a lot of emotions. A few years ago, the people who were brought as slaves weren't as advanced. They were from the forests. Maybe in the mountains where Valli and the lot came from, the people were a lot more self-aware than the others. Could it be that there were no more gypsies left in the peninsula? Come what may, Asumugi would instruct her brothers to leave the mountains alone. Intelligent people do not make good slaves. '*We'll search in the forests a little more. We should find a couple of more farmer settlements in the next two months or so. Are there no more cave people too, then?*' she wondered.

"Do you know of any settlements that live in caves? Have you seen any?"

"Where? Here?" Valli sighed.

"Before. Answer my question, Valli. Do not speak words that don't matter to me."

Wow. This bitch of a woman. "I do not know of any villages other than mine."

"So, the sun festival isn't real?"

"How do you know about that?"

"You don't question. I do not answer."

"The sun festival is just for our village."

"Do not lie, Valli. I heard from the platoon leaders. They have seen and heard about it everywhere. Where does it take place?"

"In our village. It didn't happen this year."

"That, even I know. Why do I feel like you're not telling me something, Valli? Why do I feel like the people of Kurinji have this web around them that we cannot see? What do you know that we do not?"

"We know where the good honey is. Not here though, there ain't no goddamn bees here."

The best bet Valli had for all the unanswerable questions was to play dumb. People believed her if she did that.

Everybody did, except Asumugi. She could sometimes tell that she was bluffing, but Valli couldn't care any less. For now, there were probably three things that she was worried about the most. One, what was this statue about? Two, did Karthik, or now the new 'Moorgan', know that she was here, or did he even remember her? And three, what was for lunch? She was getting hungry.

✤✤✤

Singamugan had come over to the forge in the fifth ring. It had been quite a while since he had ventured this far out from the palace. There were six royal guards dressed in black. Moorgan and his platoon of nine men stood there, dressed in the same black veil. It took a couple of minutes for Karthik to wrap his head around the reality that he was an outsider, pretending to be a Mahendrapuri soldier, who'd then been promoted as a royal guard, and was now pretending to be a normal soldier.

"Most men lavish their money on drinks and wealth and women. But not a true soldier. I heard from Moorgan, who so bravely saved Princess Asumugi and was rewarded for it. Your entire platoon died in a plague and you were the miraculous saviours. Moorgan and the nine of you. When he told me that he was going to buy this entire forge and make it private in the memory of your lost platoon, I asked him why. He said his platoon used to sheath and sharpen and repair their weapons here and would wait in long lines to get them done by the blacksmiths. This is where you as a platoon socialized, and he wanted this place to represent that. Just that. Moorgan, your platoon, and your story alone is an outstanding example that valour and loyalty are always rewarded and honoured in the city of Mahendrapuri. We're sooras, sons of the Sun God himself. Don't ever let your light die, soldiers. The forge is yours and so are your old jobs. I will speak to the platoon leaders about absorbing you into their platoons, and anyone who's interested in going back out there can simply speak to any of the platoon leaders you know. Kottravai Potri, Komagan Potri!"

"Kottravai potri, Komagan potri," the ten men repeated back in unison.

***

They were hungry. He didn't know anything but that. He didn't remember anything else from that night. He simply knew that there were two hungry animals at a considerable distance from him, snarling and growling. He could feel them amping up for him to reach the shore. Surrounded by his little cocoon of a world, his only way to know beyond it was through the little hole he was peeking from. The predators were going to leap as soon as his little world came any closer to theirs. He saw six glowing lights move towards him. He didn't know what they were. He had no clue as to where or who he was.

He heard the growls grow louder and louder. He knew he was near them, and saw an animal leap just above the pod, landing in the water right next to him. This toppled the pod, and he was beneath the water. He felt uncomfortable but continued floating above. The white animal kicked and moved towards him, but there were sudden noises. He heard people running towards him, and the last thing he saw was the six floating lights.

When he woke up, Karthik was still sitting at the gates near the Kottravai temple after work. How long had he been asleep? He had to leave for Mother Avvai's house soon. It was nearly time for the class. He had been going there for a couple of weeks now. She fed him good food and the animals around her house were gentle too. The peacocks, roosters, and deer were all so casual around the abode. Pillaiyaar got watermelons almost every day. He never called his Yaazhi with the name, but nevertheless, it was a good name.

He had too many thoughts in his head but wanted to go help Mother Avvai set up shop. So, he got on the Yaazhi and left for Avvai's. He saw a lot of poor people every day. He hadn't heard the full story but could figure out that the people working in the city, the everyday labour groups, were being forced. They were all taken away from their home grounds and were made to work in the name of sorcery. He had seen a few stranded people being used by other settlements like these up north, but the sheer magnitude of this slavery and the volume of Mahendrapuri's growth was disheartening. No citizen of Mahendrapuri seemed to have any remorse for how the slaves were treated, or how they personally treated them. All through his journey to Avvai's, he saw kids walking towards and away from her house. They were all dressed in brown rugs. How will they learn though?

Back at Avvai's abode, he saw the old woman oiling lamps, preparing for her class. She really hoped Karthik would come early that day. She had a few things to discuss with him.

It had been a couple of weeks since Karthikeyan started assisting her in setting things up for the class. He was a sweet boy, really. Just a little, what's the word, unpolished? He was just like her Moorgan, she'd tell him often. Just a lot more level-headed. Maybe he got that from all his travels. The experiences he'd had. She sighed. Maybe Moorgan would've been just as delightful if not for all the battles. She didn't get much time with him, though. Just a short twenty years, in which more than half was lent to him learning the art of war.

She was broken when her beloved Kannaayiran was taken away, dead, from the wretched battlefield. He was all she had to call family. And then he had a family of his own, and Moorgan became Avvai's life. He wasn't fully trained, was not thinking straight, and had not recovered from his father's death. He was carrying rage like never before when he walked to the ferry that day. She'd begged him not to join the army, yet he had so much anger that he just didn't listen. Moorgan, she smiled. What a fitting name Moorgan was. Such an angry young man, yet so innocent and naive.

"Aachi," Karthik called as he walked inside Avvai's abode.

"Karthikeya," the woman smiled. If she had any teeth whatsoever, they'd all show. "Where were you? Did you eat the food I gave?"

It had become a usual practice for Avvai to give him food for the night as he left. "Who knows, you might have even thrown out the food. Did Pillaiyaar eat?"

"We both ate, aachi. Give, I'll oil the lamps."

"Also, you have to stay a bit longer here today after the class. I might have guests coming over. I want to introduce you to a few people."

"Guests?"

"Ayye, nobody is coming to ask you for your hand in marriage," she said. "Although, you should get married in like a couple of years. You know, find a woman."

"Yea, right." His heart sank as the thought of Valli, and Ayya Nambi crossed his mind.

"Don't worry, I'll help you look. Although, today's visitors are equally important. We're meeting a few of the captives that I personally know of. I've called them here for them to talk to you."

"Talk to me, why?"

"Do you know children from the camps aren't allowed to speak to children from the city? The parents believe it's a lot 'safer' for their children if they didn't know what the captives' lives are like. They don't want the children of indigenous cultures to tell the children of the city about how they were uprooted from their homes. These days, the children of the city are convinced that war and slavery are the way of the courageous. Them not being able to hear the other side of the story – which is quite honestly the only 'side' of the story –

makes it a lot worse. Children being controlled by law is the peak of civilization, at least according to that stupid, big child."

"Are you talking about Soorapadhman?"

"Yes, yes."

"How do you take classes for slaves, then? Without the knowledge of the authorities?"

"No. I approached them a few years ago, when there were only about 60 indigenous children in total, in the entire city. Also, I'd prefer it if you addressed them that way. Slaves is the wrong word to use, I think. I told the people in a town hall meeting that these children need their education. I'd also just lost my son in the battle, so I got my way a lot easier than I expected. The people thought a few lectures about our culture to the young will help them 'blend in' easily."

"You don't teach them about the city's culture?"

"They don't need to know that. They are not interested in learning about the city that just trampled their places of existence to dust. A lot of people who were children when they were brought here have grown up to be fine adults. They aren't happy about whatever happened to them back when they were young at all. Speaking of young rebels, you will be meeting a few of them today."

"Who now? Rebels?"

"Moorgan, a decade ago, Soorapadhman had captured one coastal Neidhal settlement. He had one boat. A few dozen people followed him and he enslaved twenty people. Now, he has 6079 people enslaved. The number of villages that he's pillaged and the number of lives he's gambling with – Mahendrapuri and other settlements – the distress among the captives is all too much. We have got to set these people free. So, I've spent years training a handful of children, in secret."

"Aachi, believe me, I want to. I just..."

"You wouldn't fight."

Karthik just sat there. He didn't want to talk about this. Not to this woman. She'd be so disappointed.

"Karthikeya, what's the problem?"

"How are we setting them free exactly? It's not like all 6079 people will make it out alive after we've fought an army with metal weapons."

"Do you know what living is, child?"

"If you're going to tell me that dying is better than living in shackles, I'd not agree with you. Living itself is a gift."

"A gift that the palace of Mahendrapuri is coveting from countless people. Of course, I understand that running through the gates, screaming with just sticks in hand to face an army as strong as Mahendrapuri's is simply suicide. That's why I believe you can help them. You can help them strategize. I know you helped your father and your tribe hunt with ease using your formation plans. These folks could use some of it."

"How do you all speak of my life and act like it's not a big deal at all? Do you at least consider the scenario of me losing sleep over these mysterious powers that you have?"

"Oh, not everything is a mystery, Moorgan. Agathiyan told me."

"Well, how did he know? It's not like he's seen me hunt."

"Ask Agathiyan the next time you see him. Also, I must warn you, munis do not have to be everywhere physically to learn things. They have a very sophisticated network of knowledge sharing."

"Is that why you've been indoctrinated as one?"

"Oh, I'm not a muni yet. I've asked for some time. I will not accept the glory of being called a muni when the tribe I grew up with has blood on its hands. I will lay waste to this filth of an empire, stand on its fallen gates, declare that slavery and discrimination are mere tools of a coward, release every last indigineous person from this prison, and then crown myself with the privilege of being a muni. Or, I die a dumb old lady in this stupid abode." She walked outside to pet Pillaiyaar. Karthik sighed. This woman was very persuasive, he thought.

"Oh, you are yet to see the power of my persuasion, child."

"I give up."

✣✣✣

They heard the Yaazhi move and looked out. A couple of kids stood there. They were young and lean. Probably seventeen or eighteen years old. "Aachi," they bowed. Along with them stood four elders.

"*Nalla irunga!*" Avvai wished. "Come in, everybody. Please be seated. Nobody saw you coming here, did they?"

"No, amma. We still have to make it back to our camp spots unnoticed, but we can just tell them we went in search of honey. They still believe we are idiots, so we use it to our advantage," one of the elders responded.

"Okay. This is Karthik, he's the one I sent the message about. He goes by the name Moorgan. He works inside the palace as a royal guard. Karthik, these are my students. Former students, if I may. And these, Karthik, are elders from Kurinji, Neidhal and Mullai."

"Elders," one of them scoffed. "What elder am I if I just sit here when my people slave away?" His people were brought to Mahendrapuri a year ago, and he still was mourning a lot of loss.

"Don't worry. The first two years are always rough. You see them throw a dozen of your people in their bloody trenches a few times, and then you go in there a few times and lose all hope of fighting. Just like our elders have," one of the two boys interrupted.

"Hello, who taught you to talk back to your elders, man?"

"Sorry, aachi."

"You see what elders losing hope does to young children, Ayya Poovannan?"

"Mullai was everything we knew, mother. Green trees bore us the fruits of our labour. We were free. This… We don't know what to do here against enchantments and trenches and guards and money and… And you hadn't written us a note in one year. We didn't know if any help was coming. We're still asking them to provide us with a little more food for the children, and they keep telling us to stop sleeping with each other. Our kids are shunned for being born. Initially, it was different. We were insulted. It just hurt. Now, our kids are facing the brunt of their barbarism. Now, it angers us. Yet we can't do anything here. It's no fault of this kid that I am helpless and do not deserve the respect of an elder."

"Look, ayya," Karthik interrupted because his little speech was bringing back memories he did not want to think of when surrounded by people. "I know a man who spoke just like you did. I came into the city to bring them out of here. You will make it out of here. I will take you out of here."

He shouldn't be doing this. He shouldn't be giving them hope with no idea of what he was going to do to help them. But he also couldn't leave people wallowing in self-pity for no mistake of theirs.

"Well, at least we get to kick the asses of a few Palai people soon," the same teenager replied.

"That's the spirit, Kaarmegan. Always be ready for the rebellion."

"This isn't about the rebellion, amma. They want us to wrestle them, the newly recruited guards of the port."

"What? What wrestling?"

"The guards near the docks usually wrestle around the beach. I don't know, a couple of days ago they said we should be ready to randomly face them. They even called one of us for a wrestling match tomorrow. Dheeran is preparing for the fight in the camp as we speak. They're even paying us with two rice bags to fight against them."

"Did they come to you and ask? Did you people agree to fight them?"

"Yes they did and yes we did!" the teenager said with all chest and pride.

"Stupid people. Stupid, stupid people." Avvai got visibly upset.

"Yea, even we thought so. Why should they pay us to fight them? We'd kick their asses for free!"

"*You* stupid people, *you*! I'm saying *you* are stupid. Not them! Why would you fight? For food? I have food! I will give whatever I have, why fight, you fool?"

"It took you one year to call us again to even talk. We have been needing the food for quite a while now," Kaarmegan replied.

"And we want to fight them! We want to defeat these soldiers. In their place, with their friends watching, while their commands smirk at their valiant subservient from a distance and look at them. We want to push their faces into the mud, and tap them out! What a glorious sight it would be!"

"This guy will kill you," Avvai suddenly pointed to Karthik.

"What? No, I will not."

"Technically?"

"Technically, I would not fight. So no."

"But he could, alright. He could kill both of you in a fist fight. He has got that much training and experience. That's what it takes to be a soldier, and these guys you've agreed to fight, they're soldiers as well. So, don't be stupid. Call this thing off."

"It does not exactly work like that. We are not choosing to fight. However, we will enjoy it. I've always wanted to punch that stupid grin off their faces. Also, thanks for the enormous belief you have in us. Why make us train for years when you don't even have faith in us?"

"You have gotten way cockier than I remember. Not good, child. Not good at all. Now, I believe in you enough to take your people out of this hell hole in a perfectly planned and executed operation, with the guidance of elders and people like Karthikeya. But not enough to face a fully trained Mahendrapuri soldier in a wrestling match."

"I have a solution," Karthik interrupted. "But I think we are overestimating the ability of these kids to negotiate themselves out of this fight. It is not their choice, really. And kid, you may want to lay off the confidence a bit. A true soldier never underestimates his opponent. When you do not give your opponent the credit he deserves, you've already lost."

"Whatever. The only respect these Mahendrapuri scum deserve is my foot on their noses. What do you know, you're one of them, aren't you?"

"Well. Again, I have a plan. You will not be wrestling with them. I guarantee it," he turned to Avvai and nodded. "But why did you call them here though?"

"To introduce them to you!" Avvai gleamed, a little too proud. "We will make a break for it. I'll take you all out of this place. But all in good time."

"I've been hearing this same monologue for four years from you, Aachi," Kaarmegan spoke.

"Good. That means you've prepared to face the obvious adversity for four years. The more prepared you are, the closer to your goal you'll be." Karthik spoke.

"Good pep talk, man. Really means a lot coming from within the black robe that people wear when they point spears at us."

"Look, I'm not just a guy that wears black robes. I also wear red robes. Inside the castle. You don't know about the red robes, do you? A lot of things, brother. You are oblivious to a lot of bigger things outside of your anger. If you burst open the gates of Mahendrapuri and revolt, everybody will be slain to bits with metal swords. What weapons do you have anyway? I heard stone isn't allowed inside the colonies. So sticks, probably? Do you know what happens to sticks when people swing metal swords at them? They snap." He took out his sword in a swift motion and sliced the sticks one of the elders held with almost no effort at all. "That's what'll happen to plans made in haste. I'll give you the signal. Soon. I'll pass it on to your own children who come here to study. Until then, get a handful of men ready, Kaarmegan. With a few loyal men by my side, Mahendrapuri will fall, but only if we're willing to wait. Hunting is but a test of patience. *Do not fear, for I am here*"

He was serious this time. He needed people from the captive colony to trust him enough to wait. Revolts without enough ammunition would put people in grave danger.

"How long?" Kaarmegan sounded sincere. For him and his colony, these were the first words that had any sign of hope in a long time.

"Not long, Kaarmega. Not very long. Elders here, and the elders of the other clans as well, please do not let your children lose hope. I'm sorry for the state of your people now. We shall rebuild Kurinji. And every other settlement there was. The peninsula will be home to all of the clans again. The walls of Mahendrapuri aren't strong enough to keep the Thamizh clan down. We will break them down. Keep your children well-fed and men well-trained. I will send a signal when things are ready. Also, boys, not one word about me or the red robes or our plan to anyone. Even to people in the colonies. We work in silence, for now."

"Karthikeya, about the wrestling challenge from the guards?"

"I will take care of it." Karthik assured Avvai.

Valli knew she couldn't keep guessing for so long. This was a bad idea. The curiosity was gonna kill her. She should ask.

No, she shouldn't. Why should she? What does she care what the stupid statue was going to be? This woman had her entire village prisoned. But what is the statue though? She sighed.

"What is it, Valli?" Asumugi asked. "Why the sigh?"

"Nothing. This is a bad decision. I think I cannot contain my curiosity anymore. I want to know what the statue will be."

She cut out the imprisonment part from her answer, but this would do as she personally thought Asumugi was at her most vulnerable when she was sculpting.

"Oh, interesting," Asumugi replied. "I could give you clues."

"Nice!"

"We see the subject of this sculpture every day." She stopped a second, and looked up at Valli's face.

"Oh." Well, that didn't help narrow it down one bit. "Right."

"You'll see."

"Princess Asumugi, the king is here to see you!" one of her stewardesses announced as she came running and stopped right outside the studio.

"Thank you, Kannukkiniya. And good you stopped outside. Respect."

'*This woman with her condescending hammer and chisel,*' Valli thought. '*Poor Kannu. Also, what? The king?*'

"Arriving, king Soorapadhman!" the guard at the entrance announced.

"What are you doing here?"

"Get out, all of you," he shouted. The two stewardesses and the guard left the vicinity.. He stood near the entrance just like Kannukkiniya, and waited for Asumugi to let him in.

"We have a serious problem, Asumugi. The platoons that went in the direction of the Kurinji villages have written back."

"Come in," Asumugi spoke, still working on the stone. "You're talking about the two platoons that hit the sun festival, yea?"

"They've found a stash underground. Somewhere along their return route. It must be around the swamps, judging by how long it takes for the messages to reach us."

"What does the message read?"

"Underground, Mahendrapuri uniforms and weapons, soldiers nowhere." He took out a piece of dry palm leaf. "I might be reading wrong."

Asumugi stopped sculpting and took the leaf from him.

"Under the mud, Mahendrapuri uniforms, weapons, soldiers nowhere. Yea, you're right," Asumugi nodded. "Maybe some of our soldiers left it there. Also, it doesn't say how many uniforms or weapons are there. I'm guessing a couple of soldiers just kept their uniforms down, buried them along with their swords, and ran out on their platoon. We've been hearing that a lot, you know. They start feeling all guilty and mushy after they've raided their fourth or fifth village. Maybe that's what we should do. Send a soldier only three times. What do you say?" she picked up her hammer and chisel.

"So, you don't think it's serious?"

"You think it's serious? What do you think it is?"

"I don't know. I feel like they're trying to send us a message," the king sighed.

"Of course, they sent us a message. Those fools just learnt how to. Brother, you're reading too much into it," Asumugi went back to whacking the rock.

"Do you think we should at least discuss this in court tomorrow?"

"If it bothers you that much, please do. If my least paranoid brother is this shaken up, I can only imagine what frenzy this throws Singa and Tarakan into."

"What are you sculpting anyway?"

"Oh, you'll see."

She liked playing this game.

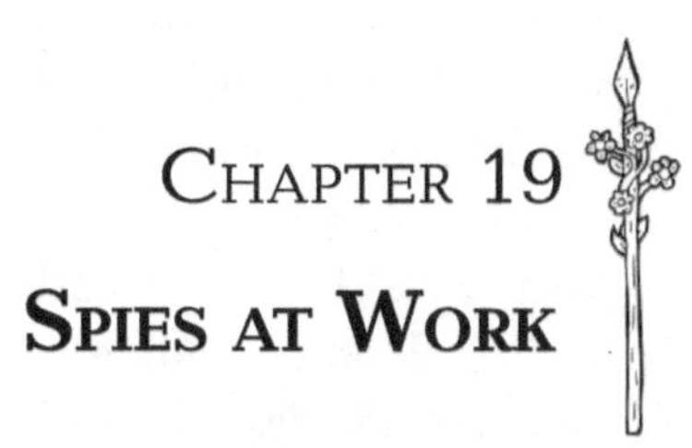

Chapter 19
Spies at Work

Karthik had just left Kadalon's tent at the beach. Kadalon was covering his new platoon member's shift at the port. He had just joined the Puliyappar platoon. He thought he could live without problems for one week, at the very least. But well, this kid just HAD to bring bad news. Who the hell was Avvai anyway? He started playing with the sand. It stopped his brain from eating itself out.

The blacksmith's shack proved to be a great investment. Both strategically, and economically. They didn't have to spend as much on chathrams. Plus, he got to see Devayanai often. She was very angry, all the time. She was still a slave by the books and couldn't even talk when the members of the platoon came to the shack. The nine of them had been 'absorbed' by four different platoons. Hence, the exclusivity didn't last very long before the favours and elitism kicked in. Just because Karthik bought it, people weren't ready to give up the best blacksmiths in town to a bunch of washed-up soldiers and miracle boys who went up the ranks by saving a woman. "Plague boys," they called them. No platoon member respected them.

Every day, he saw the people of his village through his eye slits. He saw them row ferries after ferries with weapons pressed to their back. The other day, he had seen kids from the captive camps carrying twice their weight in fish. Just a week earlier, he saw one of them fall down and the guard nudged him with his foot and said, "Go on then, don't break your fucking back." Kadalon wanted to ram a sword through the back of his neck. He couldn't. Because it would put the whole mission in jeopardy. Which was what, exactly?

He didn't know. Nobody knew. His men were losing their heads. And, of course, Karthik had to just add to this. A meeting with the princess herself at the beach tomorrow. And he wants us to wrestle if it comes down to it! How nice. Would help improve the team rapport greatly, thanks. Something crossed his vision and he looked up, immediately picking up his sword. He saw a short, stout silhouette walking towards him. It was past midnight, and there were no ferries anytime soon.

"Who's there?"

"Shhhhh. Hello, why are you shouting? I thought I made friends with the king of the sea! Kadalon, this is Agathiyan!" Agathiyan tip-toed towards Kadalon, with this finger pressed to his mouth. "Don't you shout! The Mahendrapuri soldiers aren't really welcoming of the muni clan. I can get away in the day, but at night, I can't do a lot of blending now, can I?"

"You must be crazy! The platoon leaders will literally send in all the thousand soldiers to catch a member of your clan if only they knew where you were, and you just show up at their fortress foothill and sand beach docks. How are you not dead yet?"

"I'm short, remember. People don't care about short people who're always eating something out of their sling bag."

He picked up a gooseberry and started munching on it.

"What is it?"

"Gooseberry. You want?" He offered a couple to Kadalon.

"How come you're here anyway?" Kadalon started munching on the gooseberries. This man was no joke. He sure knew how to get across places and keep an extremely low profile.

"You know, if Karthik was half as bright as you, he'd be asking the right questions, just like you. That stupid boy, always trouble. You know what though, he doesn't seek trouble. Trouble seeks him. He could literally be sleeping and he'd wake up to a bunch of wolves. I've seen that happen, actually."

"How do you know him anyway?"

"The question is, what do you know about him?"

"He's from the north, right? The snowy mountains? He is here for the Kurinji folk. He spoke a lot. Not really hard to get to know that kid. You just gotta smile and nod."

"He's from the north, yea. You know, muni folk travel a lot and we carry a lot of stories. We have a story about a child who survived a mighty flood, and beasts, and went on to live with a man who had long forgone the ideology of society. Do you have time for it?"

"I mean, it's past midnight and we're just two men sitting on the beach. Why shouldn't we talk?"

"Nice. Gooseberry?"

"No. I'm good, thanks."

"Try drinking water now!"

Kadalon was a little confused but did it anyway. He walked up to a station pot nearby and had some. What the hell!

"How does water taste so sweet after such a bitter fruit?"

"See. That's why you should always listen to Agathiyan. I know my tastes!" He picked another gooseberry and ate it.

"So, about the story?"

"Yea. Yea, the story. The story of a man who's believed to be the first person to really ever set rules for us-the muni clan. He was the first muni, if history is right. And history is but a tricky mirage of the reality behind us, so we don't for sure.

The person supposedly picked seven assistants or pupils or whatever you want to call them, and maybe gave them names or told them to pass on their actual names. That isn't really clear, but he taught them things. These were really primitive times, I tell you. Ten or fifteen generations of munis ago. He, unfortunately, did not pass on his name. But when he left his village, he took the youngest of the seven disciples with him. The story goes that this duo walked together for thousands of days, and made it to the great mountains and conquered them. The boy who travelled with him, nobody knows who he was, because his name wasn't passed on. Nobody's heard from those two again.

A few years ago, we started hearing about a curly-haired, tan young man. He was raised by a tribe up in the mountain. A very peculiar tribe, one that befriended beasts like snow leopards and yaks, and used them for hunting and rearing. The reason this piqued our interest - the aadhi muni, or the first muni, supposedly taught how to befriend beasts as one of the first lessons to his disciples.

After we started hearing too many stories, one of us went there wondering if we could trace this young man back to his roots. However, nobody in his own tribe knew who he was either. One cold night, six women and two snow leopards went to fetch water from a stream nearby and they saw a baby floating about on a chiselled log of wood. They picked him and brought him to the village, where the chief and his wife raised him as their own, they said. The damned chief had conveniently left with his wife to 'find a new home' at a place called Kashi, and wasn't there to answer any of our questions. The chief had no real ties to the village as well, and was an outsider that came about at the same age as the boy did.

So, this boy is a ghost from a place very far, with a ghost clan elder with no history, yet he somehow acts like he knows this place and is ready to lay his life down for a bunch of people he seemingly has no connection to, whatsoever.. Does anything about this whole fiasco make sense to you?"

"I… I need water. I'll go get some water. Do you want some water?"

"Damn, those gooseberries got you thirsty, huh?" Agathiyan was still eating them.

Why does this man talk with so many gooseberries in his mouth? Why does he eat so many? What did that entire story mean? How has this helped anybody? What is it about ghosts? Who is this person? Is he even sane? He continued drinking water.

"Hey so,"

"What the fuck" Kadalon jumped on hearing a voice near him.

"Hello, don't shout man. Don't get me killed yet. I have too many good recipes to share before dying. Now, listen to me carefully. Tomorrow, when you meet the princess, tell her that you saw a muni sneaking through the port at midnight. Tell her that you chased him. He tripped, fell down, and vanished, but dropped this little palm leaf. Yea? Will you tell her that? Here's the palm leaf. I'll save you the trouble of chasing me because you know, I'm short and I'm carrying one too many gooseberries to run. So, yea. Do you want any gooseberries though? I can spare a few…"

"What the hell are you on about? How do you know I'm visiting the princess tomorrow?"

"Man, you need to keep your voice and tone down! Be shocked in silence, brother. Why do you have so many questions anyway? Haven't you realized by now that this is exactly my job?"

"What job? What do you mean?" Kadalon whispered, his pitch still too high.

"Too many questions and none of them relevant. Karthik's stupidity and inquisitiveness are rubbing off on you, my friend.

Stay away from that kid. But don't though. I was just joking. Please stay with Karthik. The redemption is near, and he needs all nine of you by his side to get this done."

"What do you mean redemption?"

The muni was slowly walking away from Kadalon. He followed him.

"The rebellion, the mighty king of the seas. You are going to free your people soon. Karthikeyan is going to do it. Mahendrapuri is soon to fall."

The muni started picking up pace and was, at best, jogging.

"What the hell?" Kadalon ran behind him. "Ayya stop!" He ran behind him.

"And he still chooses to chase. Damn it!"

The muni dropped the etched palm leaf down and ran faster into the dark abyss. Kadalon picked up the palm leaf. There were a lot of symbols etched on it. Maybe with a sword or a shard stone. He couldn't read it fully, his platoon were still not through with the messaging course. He figured the message was about Kraunch. How did the Muni know how to write?

Well. What a disaster of a night this was! A defeated Kadalon made his way back to their shack well past midnight. Hell, it was closer to day than it was to night. He just had enough time to freshen up. He had to go back to the bloody beach. He prayed to the seas to give him the strength to not behead the princess in broad daylight in the middle of two Mahendrapuri platoons. He really wanted to. Why the fuck would he pass information about the locations of innocent people to a tyrant's sister? Who was this damn muni anyway? He just wanted to go fishing with the boys again. He sighed as he entered the shack.

"Let me guess. You are Avvai."

She sat there in the middle of the shack on a pile of sand. Four of his men and his sister Devayanai were sitting around her, looking up at his face with just as much confusion. Was the day not over yet? It was almost the next day!

"Kadalaane, it's good to finally meet the King of the seas."

"You know her?" Meenappan asked, sitting with his back against a pillar.

"I guess Karthik does."

"Yea, that much we know. She said she's here to help us get out of Mahendrapuri" Devayanai replied.

Kadalon sat down next to her and looked at Avvai. She grinned. "She doesn't even have teeth."

"Yea, but she says she has an army of sixty-three trained soldiers. All seventeen to twenty three year olds. I guess teeth don't matter." Thuduppan said.

"Hello, I'm old okay. When I was your age I had better teeth. I even brushed them every day. Stupid teeth fell off a few years ago," she grinned again.

"Where do you have this army that you speak of?"

"What do you plan to do with my children who hold the key to the freedom of the Thamizh Kudi is a more pressing question, don't you think?"

"You know what, I think you and the short muni would make great friends."

"We already are. He's like my son. Cute fellow no, that Agathiyan?"

✣✣✣

Agathiyan entered Karthi's place carefully. He still had sometime before the sun fully came out.

"Why do you not sleep in the blacksmith's shack? You bought the place, after all." He asked a fast asleep Karthik.

"What the hell!" Karthik sprung awake, picking his spear up. "Oh, it's, it's just you. I gotta sit down. Holy crap."

He sat down and set the spear aside. Devayanai had made a full metal spear for him. The ones the other soldiers had were made of wood with only a sharp metal edge. This thing was completely metal! It was so heavy, but one could not imagine walking unscathed from someone as skilled as Karthik wielding that weapon.

"I was barely awake, Ayya. I could've rammed the spear through your neck. Don't play with me like this." he sighed.

He stood up, peeked out of his room, and closed the entrance with a big wooden board. People usually used the *thatti* when they were changing or when they didn't want people to come inside. He figured casually holding conversations with one of the most sought-after fugitives isn't something he wanted people to see. "You never told me you were this famous in Mahendrapuri. You also didn't tell me about this place when I set out to find Valli. You didn't tell me Valli's village was going to be their next target. All you did was eat gooseberries and spit half of them on me while talking." He hadn't seen the muni since he'd joined the platoon at the Mahendrapuri palace. He'd often heard about munis and Agathiyan, in particular, since then. Cave people, cruel, ritualistic, man-eaters, satanic cult. He heard a lot about the munis inside the walls of the castle.

"If I had told you about Valli's village, you would've valiantly joined the fight. And you'd have died. If I'd told you about Mahendrapuri before you started your quest, you'd have ridden straight to the foothills of Mount Kraunch without the Neidhal men by your side. And you'd have died. The part about me being famous here, well. What concern is that of yours anyway? Even today, I had deer meat in the same chathram. Nobody seemed to care."

"Right, my bad for not wanting the army I pretend to work for to kill you."

"Gooseberries?"

"Why are you here, anyway?" Karthik wanted to be left alone. Tomorrow was going to be stressful.

"A platoon that went out to capture Kurinji settlements made it to the city almost a year ago. It came back with a bunch of people, tonnes of livestock, and a lot of information about a gathering called..."

"Sun festival?"

"Yea. I've been to the festival twice. I had to kind of leave my first one halfway, so I attended another one a couple of years ago. I particularly like..."

"Ayya, the platoon."

"Yea, yea. Sorry. So, this year, Asumugi sent two platoons to follow the tracks that lead to the Kurinji settlements."

"They're trying to bust the festival and bring the entire Kurinji here."

"I doubt if the whole of Kurinji will be here. Whoever is left after the Mahendrapuri soldiers are through with it, they might come. But, will that be the 'whole of Kurinji'?"

"We have to stop this. We can stop it, right?"

"Well, I was not finished in the first place. They found the festive grounds and caught almost all of the women, children, and elderly folk. More than half the men were slain, and the rest of Kurinji is already on their way here. As we speak, actually. They don't camp much, even during the nights."

He'd bailed on the people of Kurinji, again. Karthik was uncomfortable having this information delivered to him like this. Why did it feel like it was his fault that the army had slayed helpless men who just wanted to celebrate the sun? What did they do wrong anyway? Who are the people of Mahendrapuri to take away something as personal and superficial as freedom? Building walls, keeping people inside gates. How many Nambis died this time? How many Vallis are on their way to this hell right now? Why?

"Do you have any information that might cheer me up? Or is it all depressing news about killing and slavery and dead fucking people?"

"The Mahendrapuri soldiers did not know which settlements there were, exactly. So, they ambushed even before they made it to the festive ground. After they burnt the place down and took people as hostages, a couple of other Kurinji settlements came in. The settlements that came in late are following the tracks of an unknown enemy that raided their festival ground. So, at least a hundred soldiers are a couple of days behind the Mahendrapuri soldiers. They're not armed to their teeth, exactly. But they're a hundred good, trained hunters and warriors. So, if you can make your way to Kraunch any time in the next two days…"

"We'd have an army to back us up. You want me to rebel?"

"No. I want you to realize."

"Realize what?"

"Countless, helpless people later, there will be a day when the unfortunate many will throw themselves at the knives, swords, and spears of Mahendrapuri, to save their future generations from coming to the wretched hell this place is. I'm asking you to man up and be part of the process. With or without you, this will happen. Not tomorrow, maybe. But surely they're bound to. Help them, Karthikeya. Help my people!" The muni seemed as if he'd cry when he spoke the last sentence.

"Alright. What should I do?"

"Kill some bad people, Karthikeya."

"If it comes down to that, I will try not to flinch," Karthik sighed.

"I have to leave. The first ferry leaves in a few minutes. But remember, Kraunch is the key."

The muni threw a couple of gooseberries for Karthik to catch and walked out of the room.

CHAPTER 20

CRASHING A PARTY

"Arriving! Arriving! The king of kings, Soorapadhman is here!" The royal guard announced. Karthik was barely there. Where was the platoon, anyway? Had they crossed Kraunch? Did they find out about the people in the burrows or Kadalon?

"Arriving! Arriving! The king of the mountain, Tarakasuran is arriving!"

"Princess Asumugi and Commander Singamugan! Arriving! Arriving!"

"Council, we have here all the elders of the Palai clan, a few priests, our valiant platoon leaders, and my beloved family. We have good news, first of all. But before that, I also have something pressing to discuss. I will reserve good things for the last, and I'll open up with my concern. Asumugi, please read this out."

" 'Under the mud, Mahendrapuri uniforms, weapons, soldiers nowhere'. That's what it reads."

"This was sent by our platoons that are heading back to Kraunch as we speak. They should be here anytime this evening. We got the message last night. Why send a message at all, if this isn't as serious, and they're going to be here soon anyway?"

"I still think you're reading too much into it."

"That's part of the job description. What do you think, Singamugan?"

"I think, either way, we just have to wait until evening. Our forces are returning to touch base with us, and we can understand what they meant from them."

"That renders the fact that they sent an obsolete message even when they knew they would be arriving here in a day."

"We are just teaching these fools how to send written messages, brother. Of course, they're gonna dance around the newfound fire like cavemen." Tarakan scoffed.

"I don't know." Soorapadhman grew quiet.

"Come on, sir. Give us the good news!" Banukopan nudged.

"Alright, so be it. Just keep your troops ready to go at all times. This is irrespective of any potential threats." He pointed to Tarakan and Sinkamukan. "Gentlemen, we have hit the sun festival. The greatest settlement of all time – before us that is – the clan of the so-called Gods has been defeated. Kurinji has completely fallen! Our powers grow beyond reach every day, and it is our duty to bring the whole peninsula under the umbrella of Mahendrapuri. Our prosperity will be shared, our ways will be taught, our culture will be inculcated, but we will rule. One clan, towering over the entire Thamizh Kudi, we will be the new generation of Gods."

"But where will they live?" One of the elders asked, disregarding the prideful monologue.

"We will keep them at Kraunch for the time being. Tents are being set up at the beach for them to stay in, for when they're brought here. They can stay there for a while, and we'll make enough room for them in their neighbourhood. Mahendrapuri's inner circles will not be disturbed to accommodate a bunch of slaves, we can promise you that." Banukopan promptly responded.

"Do we all get a slave? Or is it state allocated?" an elder from the back asked.

"This time we're keeping a significant portion of them. Especially the ones who can sculpt or hunt. The state is looking to increase the size of our hunting party and build a few more monuments along the sea line," Banukopan replied.

"So, we get none of them?"

"We'll see tonight. I hope the harvest from the sun festival is as good as they claim," Soorapadhman sighed. He was just bitter that nobody took any interest in the message. His people were becoming too greedy. Well, could he blame them? It was his idea to add a few more people to the hunting party. Even he had gotten greedy. He wanted more people guarding his city, so he thought he'd take it out of the hunting front.

But what about the message? He sighed, for Sinkamukan was right; there was nothing they could do even if they wanted to. It would take a solid four hours for any of his soldiers to even reach Kraunch. To make it out of Kraunch and for them to exactly track the other platoons would take longer than the soldiers who had sent the message to come back here. Did he make a mistake? Should he have sent a few good trackers to seek their platoon out and ask what was with the message and uniforms last night itself, as soon as he got the message? Well, too damn late.

As celebrations broke out in the palace hall, Soorapadhman stormed out. Tarakan was already drunk, while Banukopan and Singamugan were discussing strategies at the back of the hall with a few elders. In the middle of the hall, a bunch of people were huddled together, overlooking a snake, dancing to the tunes of a man with a big moustache. Asumugi and Moorgan locked eyes. She signalled him to meet her out of the hall. Asumugi, along with her entourage, snuck out of an entrance. On her way out, the princess grabbed Karthik and took him to the hall outside.

"You asked if we should go to the beach?"

"Yea."

"Any occasion?"

"I heard the sun sets today."

He weirdly felt a twist in his stomach standing so close to Asumugi. She seemed so beautiful to him.

"Can I bring at least one of them?" she fanned her arms around her three slaves. She was a little more wavier and animated than usual, and all the more gigglier with Karthik.

"Whatever the princess pleases," Karthik kept his voice low.

"You're flirting with the boss's sister, Moorgan. Careful."

Asumugi then turned around and called Kannukkiniya. "Come with me. You two, leave my sight."

Karthik frowned that Valli wasn't coming along. But he didn't know what fresh hell awaited at the beach along with the wrestling soldiers and cocky teenagers, so he figured it was all for the good. "Also, whatever I please, really?" she asked.

"Yes, I guess?"

"Let's lose the veil then?"

"You're the princess. You go out there without the veil, you're gonna be the centre of attraction on the beach."

"I'm sure I am, with or without the veil."

"Well, I said what I said. Whatever the princess pleases."

Karthik was pushing this too far. But he wasn't going to reason with a drunk narcissistic woman when there were young children's lives at stake. Those soldiers would grapple the kids to death, for sure.

✣✣✣

At the beach stood a defeated, sleep-deprived, tensed, and sweaty Kadalon. He'd been waiting for more than two hours. His feet hurt, and the beach sand burnt hot. He sighed hearing the waves crashing into the city walls. That was the most depressing part of the job. Hearing the waves, but not being able to see them. Not being able to see the sea, separated by a stone fucking wall. He stiffened a little when he saw Karthik walking without his veil. With him were two women, one without a veil and the other all veiled up. *So that's the princess, then, the one with the veil?* He touched his waist to make sure that he had the palm leaf that little the muni had given him. Why the fuck wasn't this idiot wearing a veil?

"Adei, they're gonna wrestle those slave dogs. The ones who constantly gave us the looks a few weeks ago. Come see!" A guard who walked past told him.

He doesn't seek trouble though, trouble seeks him. It's really true, isn't it? All the soldiers were huddled up near a palm tree. A few people with brown dresses tried getting nearer to the huddle but the soldiers pushed them away. This was no wrestling. Those people were gonna beat them up to a pulp. He didn't know if there was a Neidhal kid in there. He didn't want to. He could not afford to keep cover in front of the fucking princess if he knew. But he had to go near to see what the princess and Karthik were up to.

The duo walked past him, and Karthik found Kadalon standing on the agreed spot. Kadalon followed the duo towards the wrestling huddle. A lot of people were noticeably walking towards it.

"What's that all about?" the woman without the mask asked Karthik. Holy shit, this was the princess then! Slaves don't talk to soldiers, and this meant that the woman without the veil was the princess. But then, who was the woman in the veil?

"I don't know. Want to check it out? We still have some time before the sun starts setting," Karthik shrugged. He didn't like the way Asumugi looked at him.

"Well, if you want to. I'd like people to know that I'm here as well. Let's see if some other motherfucker's looking to kill me. I badly want to see you fight again." Asumuki touched Karthik's arms and ran her fingers down his forearm.

"I love the positive attitude you approach life with." He held her hand and locked fingers.

Kadalon was fuming. Karthik was definitely pushing his luck. With the princess? Flirting? With no masks? Why did this kid not believe in the concept of staying undercover?

"Move please," Asumugi announced from behind a bunch of soldiers. They turned around, and a few of them realized it was the princess herself! Oh, looking at her without her damn veil; how much the men of Mahendrapuri missed this. In the last four or five years, the royalty had distanced themselves a lot, and Asumugi had started veiling up a couple of years ago.

A lot of soldiers pushed a lot of buttons and pulled a lot of strings up the management for even an errand at the palace, simply to see her. A lot of them didn't even know her, yet stood still nevertheless.

"Move, brother. Move."

Karthik cleared a path for her, and she held her head a little higher than usual, walking through the walls of a dozen Mahendrapuri soldiers. "What's the ruckus, brothers?" Karthik asked.

"We're wrestling. Our platoon leader has asked us to practise during free time."

"All of you are free?" Asumugi asked, fanning around her. There were at least thirty soldiers around. "I thought we were guarding the beach!"

"It is a special match, so..." one of the soldiers trailed off and looked down.

"Special? What kind of special?"

"We're fighting them!" the soldier in the centre of the huddle spoke, gleaming with pride.

"What?" Asumugi looked at the settlement kids. Just two of them, a little tall but definitely young. "But, they're just children."

Okay, Karthik was right. He believed in Asumugi to do the right thing, and she did.

"Why the fuck would you fight a couple of children and waste everybody's time?"

"We're not children!"

'*Damn it, what did I tell these kids!*' Karthik thought. He kept a straight face though. Kadalon was relieved that the kids weren't from Neidhal, but realized how dumb the idea was. The soldier was twice as old as the kid he was planning to fight.

"Do not talk to the princess!" A soldier hit him from the back with the blunt edge of his spear.

"You know what, you guys are losers. Get lost, everyone. Nobody's fighting anybody. Go do your fucking jobs," Asumugi yelled.

"How would we practice then? Wrestling the same people again and again is boring, and *they*'re not that friendly with us either," the soldier geared up to fight responded.

"So you want a fight?" she stepped forward.

'What the hell!' Karthik pulled Asumuki closer.

"Wait, princess. Let me," He was not letting his boss's sister drunk-wrestle a soldier without a veil on the beach.

"Even better!" Asumugi winked. Karthik walked to the front.

"I don't want to do this, princess." The Mahendrapuri soldier seemed worried about getting fired. Or worse, getting thrown in the dungeon.

"I thought you wanted a fight," Asumugi said, as Karthik walked into the centre of the huddle.

"Alright then," he looked at Karthik "You escaped a plague to die on the beach, I guess." The soldier was a couple of inches taller than Karthik. "Let's see if you really are that angry, Moorgan!"

He jumped on Karthik, tackling him down in the mud.

Karthik wasn't ready, but the moment he hit the ground, his instincts kicked in.

He slipped a mean punch the soldier was going to throw and moved his upper body to the right. With his right elbow, he landed a blow on his opponent's jaw and put an arm around him to quickly put the soldier on top, in a choke hold, while his legs wrapped around his hips. The soldier quickly barrel rolled and brought Karthik above him, pushing him over to the side. Both sprung up on their feet. They locked shoulders and positioned themselves for another round. While pushing against each other, the Mahendrapuri soldier bent down to grab Karthik's feet. Karthik jumped up a little, rolled over the soldier's back, and caught his hip. Karthik landed down safely with his legs plopped down, but his body weight threw the soldier down on his back. It was a brilliant front drop suplex, and the soldiers around the pit cheered. Karthik got on top and feigned a punch to the right and when the soldier moved to the left, he dropped his left elbow right on his forehead.

"What a fucking shot!" someone from the crowd cheered. He was so nimble, so light on his feet. Yet he threw jabs with his whole body. The people at the front heard a thud every time Karthik dropped a punch or an elbow. Asumugi was more than impressed. To watch him fight, for her, was like poetry in motion. No statue could capture this, she thought, yet she only wanted to make more of it.

By this time, the Mahendrapuri soldier was bleeding a lot and Karthik stopped hitting. The crowd wasn't amused but

Karthik stood up, breathless, and shook his hand down. Blood dripped down a little. "We're done. He's down," he said, out of breath.

"He hasn't tapped out yet!" one of the soldiers shouted.

"I'm not beating up a fallen man," Karthik pushed the crowd aside and stepped out of the circle of soldiers for some air. He could smell the blood. It repulsed him. How familiar the scent of human blood was. He hated it. His head spun a little from all the hard fall, so he thought he'd sit down.

"You will fight me, you bastard! I am an Asura! I am Panayan Poovasuran, and you will fight me till I fucking breathe!"

The soldier ran up to him and kicked Karthik down.

"That's enough! It was just a fun wrestling match. He's right to have stopped fighting. He'd kill you anyway," Asumugi walked up to Karthik and helped him up. "Next time, come over to the palace if you need people to fight with. Don't go to the settlement camps. They're slaves, not punching bags."

She watched the boys who stood a little afar, still looking at Karthik.

"Well, what a fight, Moorgan," Asumugi looked at Karthik. The soldiers left, one after the other, clearly upset about the fight getting stopped.

"I was not planning on breaking a man's mouth today."

"What were you planning on then?" Asumugi stopped walking and noticed a soldier still following them. "Do you want to wrestle too?"

"No, my highness," Kadalon shook his head. "I bring a message."

"Oh, you newly learnt soldiers and your messages! What the hell is it?"

"Not mine, Princess. Our platoon hasn't learnt to write fully yet. We're scheduled for a beginner's class soon."

"Who's message is it then?" Asumugi stiffened a little through all the foggy drinks she had in her system.

"From a muni."

Asumugi stopped dead in her tracks. Karthik turned towards Kadalon immediately and realized there was more to the day than they'd planned.

"I saw someone suspiciously loitering on the beach. I tried to catch him, yet he slipped. He would match the profile of a few munis we're looking for. I even caught him once. He was a little too slick and after a couple of minutes of chasing him, I realized he'd vanished into thin air, more or less. But I managed to find this on the ground. This was definitely his."

"Your name?" Asumugi put her hand out for the message. Kadalon was about to give her the palm leaf. He saw the veil of the slave near Asumugi move a little in the breeze.

"Kannukkiniya?" Shit. "Is that you?"

It had been three fucking years! Kadalon removed his veil, dropped to his knees, and fell flat on Kannukkiniya's feet in one defeated motion. The suddenness of this revelation left him wide open, with no sense of reality whatsoever. He'd seen his love. He could die in peace.

"Amma, forgive me! Forgive me, Kannukkiniya! Forgive me, for I have left my precious woman to slave away."

"Kadalon, is that you? Is that you, oh, the lord of the seas?" Kannukkiniya could not believe herself. "Kadalaane?" she screamed again, dropped to her knees, and picked Kadalon's face up. They kissed in the middle of the beach. Kadalon in his soldier's outfit, Kannukkiniya in a slave's.

Asumugi, Karthik, the soldiers, slaves, and the people on the beach just watched. Everyone grew absolutely silent, and if not for the waves crashing on the stone walls, they'd hear only the two crying lovers kissing each other.

"What the fuck is happening?" she caught Kannukkiniya and yanked her up.

"Get your fucking hands off her!" Kadalon drew his sword out and swung it. Asumugi, even drunk, was quick to pull herself out of the sword's range, but it did get her. The bridge of her nose was now bleeding. It was a very small cut, yet everybody understood that if she had just stood there, it'd have gone through her skull like butter. A couple of Mahendrapuri soldiers threw themselves at Kadalon and he pulled Kannukkiniya behind him. Kadalon started fending them off, and more soldiers were rushing in.

"What the fuck is happening?!" Asumugi asked, now holding the bridge of her nose with a piece of cloth. Karthik had no fucking clue what to do. He was NOT PLANNING ON FUCKING KILLING PEOPLE when he woke up, God-damnit. He pulled a knife and did what he could think of momentarily to stop the carnage.

"Drop your weapons or I'll slice the princess's head off!" he screamed, with a knife to Asumugi's neck.

"What?" Asumugi asked, shocked.

"Now, what did the message from muni Agathiyan read?" he asked, pressing the knife ever so slightly into the neck of the princess. The entire platoon at the beach had dropped their weapons, although a few of them were slowly inching towards Karthik, hoping they'd catch him off-guard. Karthik turned his back to the side of the stone wall while Kadalon, with a sword, stood beside him. The four of them slowly moved towards the beach. "Read it." Karthik screamed into Asumugi's ears.

"Infiltrated Kraunch. Men in Kurinji cluster," Asumugi stuttered, and spoke softly "Moorga? You would betray us?"

"I'm sorry, Asumugi," Karthik whispered.

"I want the young boys from the settlement camps that know how to fight!" he screamed at the top of his lungs. He saw two dozen hands go up. "Collect the Mahendrapuri weapons and come stand near me!"

They kept inching towards the beach and the docks, away from the soldiers and the crowd.

In a few seconds, there stood almost two dozen young men behind him and Kadalon with loads of weaponry.

"Any men of yours work at the beach at this hour?" Karthik asked Kadalon.

"No" He was now coming back to his senses. The cover. The plan. All of it was gone.

"Nothing then."

He turned to the boys. "Karmeegan, go to Aachi's place and tell her what happened. The rest of you, follow me. If any of those Mahendrapuri soldiers move a muscle, give me a signal and I will lay waste to their precious princess."

He showed her neck off and Asumugi was now feeling a little pressure on it. She tried struggling but couldn't. Karthik's hold was too tight. "Stop fighting, Asumugi. Please!" he pleaded in a very low voice.

When she imagined he'd be whispering things to her in the evening and would be holding her tight, this isn't what she'd envisioned. The alcohol, the nose bleed, the shit show at the beach. All of it took a toll and her breath started getting way too short and frantic.

"Come on, come on, to the beach!" Karthik and his entourage moved to the beach, and the soldiers there dropped their weapons as well. One of them cried out, cursing Karthik for hurting their princess.

"Kadalon, load up a ferry. We're going to Kraunch," Karthik resolved. Asumugi's breathing didn't stop but was now just muffled sounds.

"You," Karthik pointed to a soldier and called him forward. The boys and Kadalon were loading the ship with weapons and some supplies. "Burn all the other ferries," he said. There were five ferries camped at the dock and they needed to burn them all down.

"Fuck off."

The soldier was disgusted.

"Do it, or your princess is dead meat, motherfucker."

He pointed to Asumugi, who stood with swords around her, held by little boys. She was unconscious now and was just lying down in one corner of the ferry. Karthik saw her face. Her eyes closed, too tired and bloody. But he had to use her as a hostage. The ferries had to be burnt. They had to do this. Otherwise, the entire Mahendrapuri army was gonna come for them in a matter of hours. "Take a piece of cloth and hold her bleeding nose, will ya?" he asked one of the boys.

"Kadalon, help these fuckers burn all their fucking ferries. Maybe leave one."

He regretted asking to leave a ferry immediately, but he had to. He had to negotiate to drop the natives off, lot after lot. He knew Soorapadhman enough. He'd agree to do the trade, but would Singamugan be okay? Tarakan? Or even Banukopan? He felt strange. All this wasn't meant to happen. There was no fucking plan. He was leading a lot of men to their death. One wrong move and this whole thing would fall apart and end very badly.

"Wait, take a few of the boys with you. You, soldier scum, you do anything to my men, I will unleash it ten-fold on the city of Mahendrapuri."

He meant it, and that scared him.

A lot of Mahendrapuri soldiers were cooped up on the beach, and Karthik guessed the message was already on its way to the castle. He trusted the bureaucracy to slow down the information but knew he didn't have a lot of time either. "Kadalaane, hurry the fuck up. Get it done now!"

In a few minutes, he started seeing smoke and smelling fumes. The palm bark still provided wonderful fuel. "Thankfully they had just brought in some fresh coconut oil. There were two barrels of it. We have just set three of the five ferries aflame. I'm bringing along some oil and a flintstone, just in case," Kadalon paused. "I'm sorry, Karthik. I screwed up."

"Well, a little too late to realize. I'm really not in the mood, Kadalon. Help me get these kids and Asumugi to Kraunch. We'll have to plan our way out of Mahendrapuri during our little ferry ride. Set the fucking sails," Karthik shouted, for the waves were a bit louder and heavier than usual.

The ship had barely moved with the bunch of teenagers, Karthik, Kadalon, Kannukkiniya, and the princess when they saw a platoon of Mahendrapuri soldiers armed to their teeth run at them from the far end of the beach. They were just getting out of the dock gates. A few of them hung back, walking, dragging someone out. Shit! Kaarmegan. Karthik screamed and leaped out of the ferry but Kadalon caught him and threw him on the deck.

"Stay down, brother. There are at least a hundred men out there."

"I will kill them, I will kill every single one of them. I sent that boy out! I have to save him." His sole mission for the day was to save that one fucking child. Not all this tomfoolery.

"Hold him, boys," Kadalon screamed as he ran to Karthik and kept him down. It took six of them to keep him down for a couple of minutes. The Neidhal boys were keeping the sails up and the boat floating. The ship had sailed away from the shore. When they finally let him go, all the men at the beach were just a distant mirage, the size of a little finger. He saw a bunch of pinkies swimming into the sea. What were they planning anyway? Swim the whole day to rescue one woman? They probably would, who's he to say? He also saw a bunch of pinkies gather around something. Probably Kaarmegan. Why did he send him? He'd killed someone. He saw people slaughtering a teenager because he didn't think straight in the heat of the moment. He didn't feel any pain. It was all but a distant memory, that beach. He was going to Kraunch, and they'd probably kill a bunch of people there too. Soldiers at the mountain. He didn't want to believe it, but it seemed like he had just started a war. The soldiers had just assassinated a young boy on the beach. The natives were gonna fight. They were going to get slaughtered. The full wrath of the Mahendrapuri army was going to rain down on Kraunch; if need be, everybody would swim across the *aazhi* to save the princess. What will he do with just a bunch of under-trained boys? He missed Pillaiyaar. Thank God he'd fed him. He was stationed at the palace, so he'd be fed well. He guessed that they'd never let Kaarmegan reach Avvai's place, so it was going to take a little while before she figured anything out. At least he didn't mention her name. Or did he? He didn't know. He walked to the edge of the boat and stared into the horizon. Mahendrapuri was beginning to sink into the abyss. The night was falling. Asumugi was not bleeding anymore, but she didn't wake up either. Kadalon and whatever his fucking girlfriend's name was stood on the other side of the ferry. He didn't have it in him to even think about if he'd ever see Valli again. His head was full of a gazillion questions and he had answers to almost none of them. The worst part? If he'd simply not wanted some honey, he wouldn't have been a part of any of this. He remembered the cave painting. He didn't remember a lot, though. He remembered the blue expanse. He didn't know what a sea was back then, but now, he knew.

"Mother Ocean is the kindest, for she gives us food; but she is also the fiercest, for she's unfathomably deep! Oh kindest, oh fiercest!" The Neidhal boys sang in voices, faded by the sound of the sea.

Kraunch is the key. What did he mean by Kraunch was infiltrated?

"So, he gave this to you?" Karthik asked Kadalon, holding out the muni's message. Kannukkiniya's cheeks were dry and itching, and she wasn't sure if it was from the tears or the sea.

"Yes. He gave it to me yesterday."

"And he told you to give it to Asumugi?" Karthik turned around to see if Asumugi was still asleep. Or unconscious. Or whatever the fuck she was. There was no movement from her at all, except for the occasional heaving and whispers.

"Yes. I didn't know what was in it, anyway. I knew it was about Kraunch, nothing more."

"You didn't care to ask?"

"Brother, that man told me nothing. He just ran and vanished into thin air as soon as I started asking questions."

"Sounds like Agathiyan," Karthik sighed. "What does this mean though?"

"Maybe he has a few men in Kraunch. I heard rumours about the army capturing a lot of people at the sun festival. A few of them might be munis."

"There's probably an army of Kurinji men coming Kraunch's way. I know that. But, why would he want that information to reach Asumugi? And essentially, the royalty?"

He sat near the passed-out Asumugi for some time. For a moment, he forgot that she kept Valli slaving away. He forgot that she was the tyrant's sister. All he saw was a beautiful young woman who'd paid the price of a bad situation.

"We see Kraunch."

He heard the Neidhal boys call out.

If he walked two dozen teenagers, his good-for-nothing friend, his cry baby girlfriend, and a princess with a bleeding nose into Mount Kraunch, the two platoons there would tear their team apart. He ran up to the front of the boat.

"Bring the sails down. We need to hang back here for a little longer."

"What?" Kadalon walked up to him.

"What? There're at least a hundred soldiers at Kraunch. I'm not walking in there with a suicide squad."

"So, how long do you plan on staying in the middle of the ocean? What exactly is your plan?"

"The plan is to lower the sails. And set them on fire."

"What now?"

✣✣✣

In a couple of minutes, the sails were down. Kadalon climbed up the sail beam and poured a little oil, setting the sail in flames. He jumped down, and watched the fire kick in. "We probably have twenty minutes until the boat starts losing its integrity."

"And it's only 5 minutes from here to Kraunch, yea?"

"Yea. I hope you're right. I hope this works."

"Gear up!" Karthik yelled.

His plan had worked. A ferry started from Mount Kraunch towards their boat, and they had torches as well. The flame lights coming towards them brought back memories of the six lights near the river to Karthik. He shook it off and checked his gear. He still had his metal spear. They kept shouting, asking if everyone was okay. Karthik and the gang kept making noises as if they were in an emergency. Which was true, frankly.

The ferry came nearer by the minute, and the men on Kadalon's boat were amping themselves up for a furious battle. "Somebody tell me what the fuck is going on or I'll slice every man on this goddamn boat!"

They heard Asumugi. She shook a little beaten up and she was tired. The fire and heat and the sound had woken her up from the blood-loss slumber. The blood on her nose had just clotted, and she was furious. She had picked up a couple of swords from the deck, and stood there swaying.

"Well, there's always a certain timing in this woman," Karthik muttered and looked back at the fast-approaching ferry. What was the plan now?

Kill some bad people, Karthikeya!

Chapter 21

Guessing Game Ends

Soorapadhman walked up to his sister's forbidden art room. He gently removed the *thatti,* or the wooden plank, and entered. The statue she had been working on the day before was covered with a red silk cloth. He hated his sister because she callously used iron and silk to carve mere stones, but didn't have the courage to speak to her as though her art didn't matter. It really did, though. Her art adorned every street of the city and every part of the palace. Still, did she have to use silk? A simple rug wouldn't do? Weren't stone carving tools enough? Did she have to blacksmith them out of whatever iron they had left?

He hated that the city was already depending on the pesky foreign rats for iron. Any day now, they could pull up on the shore with a few dozen boats, with men armed to their teeth, and he'd have no lines of defence except for the big stone wall and a few brave soldiers. He didn't want to lose either. He heard Tarakan singing in his ungodly awful voice from the floor beneath. He sighed. Why did he let people bring in drinks anyway? They'd captured just the clan of Kurinji, not Gods themselves.

He walked up to the far end of the room, beyond the big red veil. There sat the ten-foot idol, with its shoulders and head covered. Even without the face, this version of Kottravai gave him the chills. He felt guilty for even standing there, in front of a woman who personified pure anger. An unadulterated essence of Mother Kottravai. He took a deep breath and pulled down the silk cloth covering the idol.

Her skinny face, the long tongue, her prominent collar bones, her lanky build, her eyes, uncovered breasts, and the skull crown on her head. Everything really embodied what Mother Kottravai's stories told she was like. They just didn't have it in them to keep this in the temple. So, they had to soften it up. His sister was truly an artist. What had she been sculpting yesterday anyway?

He walked up to the sculpting table and removed the cloth. Until yesterday, the part above the hip had just chunks of cut-out rocks with space to carve the upper body out. Even now, the statue still had very little details to it. No dresses added, no hair, no muscle definition. It was just a bald, burly man with a spear in his hand. His stand was wonky, with some of his weight leaning onto the spear. Was it a man? It had to be. The proportion added up.

Where was Asumugi anyway? She wasn't the one to party with her brother. In fact, when he came upstairs, he'd come in hopes that his sister would be back in some time as well, and they could discuss a few possible places of accommodation for these Kurinji folk. The elders were right, though. The town already had a lot of people in it. Not planning it right would be detrimental. He was hoping to meet his sister there.

He decided to go check her room. He put the clothes back where they were, kept the *thatti* back, and went up to her room. "Asumugi!" he called out from the *thatti* in front of her room.

"Who's there?" Valli asked from the other side. She was already sulking that Karthik and Asumugi had gone to the beach. They weren't even wearing masks, and they were too damn flirty.

"The king," Soorapadhman removed the *thatti*.

"Oh, sorry," Valli wasn't really going to let this big man make her any more anxious than she already was. Should she rat them out? Well, the least she could do to get revenge. "The princess has gone to the beach!" she announced.

"What?" This little brat of a woman! "With whom?"

"Ka… I mean Moorgan!" She shouldn't rat him out yet though; maybe if he kissed the princess tonight then she'd rat him out, that flirty bastard.

"This woman does not listen to me! At all!" He stormed out of Asumugi's room and went downstairs.

"Hey, brother! Come dance!" Tarakan pulled him. Soorapadhman was not in the mood really. He walked past him to the palace entrance and called a few men. He just wanted them to keep an eye on her, but not spook her. As the men were leaving, he saw a few soldiers break in and run inside. They were dressed in black veils, so they obviously didn't belong here. The guards at the gate chased them with their weapons drawn, but he told them to stand down.

"What happened? Why the hurry?" he asked the heavily breathing group of six soldiers.

"Moorgan! Moorgan took the princess away on a ferry!"

"What now?" Soorapadhman's voice suddenly grew way deeper and his big right hand was already gripping that poor soldier's neck.

www.ingramcontent.com/pod-product-compliance
Lightning Source LLC
La Vergne TN
LVHW041212150826
845673LV00001B/367

* 9 7 9 8 8 8 6 8 4 6 9 7 3 *